D1172962

KITE
IDENTITY

Also by Harry Edge

Spray

KITE
IDENTITY
BOOK ONE SOFT TARGETS

HARRY EDGE

Hodder
Children's
Books

A division of Hachette Children's Books

A Catalogue record for this book is available
from the British Library

ISBN 978 0 340 98833 6

Typeset in Baskerville by Avon DataSet Ltd,
Bidford-on-Avon, Warwickshire

Printed in the UK by CPI Bookmarque Ltd, Croydon CR0 4TD

The paper and board used in this paperback by
Hodder Children's Books are natural recyclable products
made from wood grown in sustainable forests.
The manufacturing processes conform to the
environmental regulations of the country of origin.

Hodder Children's Books
A division of Hachette Children's Books
338 Euston Road, London NW1 3BH
An Hachette Livre UK company

This one's for Georgina

With thanks to Sue, Allison and Emily

Soft Target **noun**: *a person or place said to be relatively unprotected and vulnerable — e.g. to terrorist attack*
Dictionary.org

PART ONE

One

BROOKLYN

New York in mid-June must be the best place in the world to turn sixteen. School is closed for the summer and it's hot enough to wear shorts. Luke was determined to have a good time. Easier to do if his dad had remembered what day it was. Or his sister. OK, Megan was somewhere in Scotland, taking final exams. She had an excuse. Dad, on the other hand, had an office in New York. Yet Luke was lucky if he saw him twice a year. It was complicated, Dad said.

But not all that complicated, when you knew the score. The way Mom told it, Luke was the result of a rebound relationship. Crystal, his mother, wanted him. Jack Kite didn't. Jack paid child support but was never around for long. He dipped in and out of Luke's life at irregular intervals. Megan made more contact than Jack did. When Luke grew up, Jack said, he'd understand. He and Luke would have a man to man.

Sixteen was grown up, wasn't it? Today was as good a time as any. Luke got out his cell and called Kite Industries' New York office.

'Put me through to Jack Kite, please.'

The operator drew breath before employing her sing-song voice. 'And who would be calling?'

'His son, Luke.'

'Putting you through to Mr Kite's personal assistant.'

The phone was answered by somebody named Francis.

'I'm sorry. Your father is on his way to the UK at the moment. Is there some kind of a message I can—'

'Forget it,' Luke said. 'I'll get him on his cell.'

He hung up. Luke was screwed, again. Luke didn't have Dad's cell number. They weren't close enough. But Dad would fly over the pond to be with precious Megan at the end of school.

Luke's phone vibrated, indicating an incoming text. He checked the window. It was his sister – sorry, half-sister. Scotland was five hours ahead, which meant she was just coming out of her final exam. Megan wished him a happy birthday and asked what presents he got. Luke didn't want Megan to know that Dad had let him down. He texted back: BIKE OFF 4 RIDE.

A moment later, Megan replied: HEY! ME 2 ENJOY. That was Megan, healthy in body and mind. Luke wasn't big on bike riding. It was something he only did on holiday. If Jack Kite had bothered to ask, he would have known not to buy him the bike for last year's birthday.

Luke had to get out of the apartment, though. And this was a holiday, even if he was spending it at home. Maybe a bike ride wasn't such a bad idea. Luke changed into shorts then collected his bike from the lobby of the apartment building. In the sticky afternoon heat, he set off towards

2

Prospect Park. He was half a mile from home when he heard an explosion.

SCOTLAND

Megan and Grace cycled out of school in the June sun.

'Who were you texting?' Grace asked.

'Luke. It's his birthday.'

'You never talk about your brother,' Grace observed.

'They're not very interesting, are they? Younger brothers.'

'He still lives in New York, with his mum?'

Megan nodded. The awful Crystal.

'When did you last see him?'

'Christmas before last. When my mum died, he sent me a nice note. We keep in touch.'

'Of course you do. He's family.'

'How's Ethan?'

'Still in Africa. He hardly ever writes. Claims they don't have the internet where he is, but I don't believe him.'

Megan used to have a crush on Grace's older brother back when she was fifteen. She'd snogged him once, at the Thompsons' Christmas party. The term after that, she'd written him a couple of enthusiastic letters. He hadn't replied to either of them. Megan took that very personally at the time. But if Ethan's gap year behaviour was anything to go by, he didn't like writing letters to anyone.

The two girls began to climb a steep, winding hill. At the crest of the hill there was a tree with a large mirror attached to it. Drivers on either side could see oncoming traffic.

Otherwise they might be tempted to overtake when there was something coming. At the moment that they passed the mirror, Megan saw her and Grace's reflection. Hard to tell the two of them apart. Each had long, brown hair, although Megan's had a reddish tint. Each wore shorts, a bike helmet and a red school sweatshirt. Not for much longer though. Today's was their last exam. From now on, Megan could dress as she wanted. She was looking forward to her gap year. When she went to uni, she would no longer be the youngest girl in her class.

The girls heard a car coming, so moved into single file. Megan glanced behind. A pale-blue, four-door saloon appeared at the top of the hill, hogging the middle of the road. Seeing the girls on bikes, the car swerved towards them, rather than away.

'Look out!' Megan yelled to Grace, who was behind her. Too late. The car hit Grace. It would have hit Megan, too, but she flung herself into the ditch at the side of the road. Only now did the blue car's brakes squeal and shudder. Megan lay in the ditch, with her bike on top of her. She was hurt in several places, but she'd broken bones before and this didn't feel as bad. It was Grace she had to see to.

Shoulder aching, Megan pushed the bike up and away from her. The wheels were bent and the ditch was narrow. She couldn't get out. Where was the driver from the car? Why hadn't he come to help? Megan could hear Grace moaning, nothing else. Then she heard car wheels, skidding on grass. Was the driver trying to get away?

Grace was splayed out on the side of the road. The pale-blue saloon was backing down the grass verge towards her.

Its left wing was dented where it had sideswiped the mirror tree. Megan got a glimpse of the driver, who was staring at Grace. A middle-aged white man. The look on his face was not one of concern. He wasn't trying to help, Megan realized.

The car reversed more quickly. Could the driver not see that he was about to run over Grace? Did he mean to kill her?

There are times when you find energy you didn't know you had. Megan knew that from playing sports, but she'd never had an adrenaline rush like this before. She heaved her bike out of the ditch, into the path of the reversing car. Dead centre. She saw the driver's surprised, angry grimace. The car crunched Megan's bike before suddenly stopping. Megan hoped for a moment that she'd jammed it up. Then the car moved forward, clear of the bike. Megan heard a loud engine. Another car was coming. The dented blue saloon accelerated down the hill. If Megan hadn't been in shock, she might have noticed its registration number, but she didn't think of that until the saloon was already out of sight. She hurried to her friend.

BROOKLYN

Luke used to enjoy biking the couple of times he visited Dad and Megan for countryside vacations. In big cities, however, you had to learn to ride defensively, acting like every vehicle was about to run into you. Not such fun. Luke was nearly at Prospect Park, which had wide bike lanes and no cars, but he was sweaty and out of breath and already sorry that Megan had put the idea of biking into his head in the first place.

The traffic began to back up. Luke was able to weave in and out of stationary cars. This was more like it. He swerved around the Brooklyn Public Library then had to stop for lights. The old fashioned letters above the door read: *WHILE MEN HAVE WIT TO READ AND WILL TO KNOW – THE DOOR TO LEARNING IS THE OPEN BOOK*. Corny. Luke had been inside the library once to check out the Young Adult section. The place was full of security guards and the only reading matter of interest was a bunch of Manga novels. He preferred the public library near MOMA, with its DVDs, fast computer terminals and plentiful magazines. But Manhattan was a long subway ride away.

The traffic set off. Luke was almost in the park when an SUV jumped the lights and swung in front of him, then sounded its horn. The SUV skidded to a halt. Luke hit his brakes but the big car was hard to avoid. He had to bounce on to the curb so that he didn't hit its bumper.

'What the . . . !' His string of insults got even louder when he recognized the driver. Mom wound down her window and waited for her son to stop cursing.

Crystal Jennings was thirty-seven but had had so much work done that, in a certain light, she could pass for thirty. Luke hated the way Mom looked. Since he'd been old enough to talk, she'd tried to get him to call her by her first name so people would assume that she was his big sister or something. Sometimes he obliged.

'Throw your bike in the back,' Mom said. 'We're going to the UK.'

'Why?'

'I'll explain later.'

'Don't I need to pack?'

'We can buy what you need. Come on, get in.'

Luke did as he was told. If Mom was promising to spend big money on him, it could only mean one thing: Dad was paying. Mom might be ticked off with the sudden change of plan, but it looked like Jack Kite hadn't forgotten his sixteenth birthday after all.

Mom never talked when she was driving and Luke knew better than to distract her. Crystal was a bad enough driver at the best of times. This afternoon, she was as tense as he'd ever seen her. They got to the airport in time to make a flight that would reach London early the next morning. Mom put the car in short stay and collected the tickets she'd booked on the net. They joined the check-in line.

'How long are we going for?' Luke asked.

'I'll tell you later.'

'Where are we staying?'

'When we arrive, it'll be morning in London.'

That was one of Mom's more annoying habits, answering a different question to the one he'd asked.

'Will Dad be there to meet us at Heathrow?' Luke asked, after they'd cleared all the security checks.

'Sweetie, you'd better sit down,' Mom said. 'There's something I need to tell you about your father.'

SCOTLAND

The medics wouldn't let Megan accompany Grace to the hospital. Instead, she was summoned to the head teacher's office. Megan had been in the office once before. Two years ago, she'd hacked into a bully's email account and sent a fake confession to her entire address book. OK, maybe 'bully' wasn't quite the right word. Tessa Colgate had been giving Grace a hard time about her mother, who was in the news a lot, and Megan couldn't stand to see her friend upset. There was little physical bullying at Brunts – hardly surprising, since so many of the girls had bodyguards. People messed with each others' minds instead.

That day, the head had given Megan a good dressing down and a first warning. This afternoon, entering the oak-lined room, Megan couldn't help but feel that she was in trouble again.

'Sit down, dear,' the head, Mrs Duncan, said. 'You had quite a shock earlier. That was a terrible accident.'

'It wasn't an accident,' Megan said. 'The car knocked Grace over on purpose, then deliberately backed into her. Are the police coming to interview me? Is that why I'm here?'

There was something about the head's expression that put Megan on high alert.

'The police may want to interview you,' Mrs Duncan said. 'I'm sure they'll find the car. But I doubt that it was deliberate, Megan. You were in shock when you saw what you thought you saw. Why would anyone want to run Grace over?'

'Because her mum's in the government?'

'That's true, but . . .' Mrs Duncan's voice trailed off. She poured a glass of water from a crystal decanter and handed it to Megan. This is about me, Megan realized, not Grace.

'I'm afraid I have some bad news about your father.'

Two

LONDON

Luke and Crystal disembarked at Heathrow just before five a.m.

'Was he flying here when he died?' Luke asked.

'No. To the City of London airport,' Crystal said.

'I suppose he was on his way to see Megan.'

'I don't know. Isn't she in Scotland?'

All of his life, Luke had been jealous of Megan. She had Dad. He didn't. When her mother died, he'd been hopeful. Maybe his mom and dad would get back together. It took him a few months to find out that the world didn't work that way. In the last year, as he got over losing his wife, Jack Kite began to date models and movie stars ten years younger than Crystal. He didn't try to catch up with Luke. Luke saw more of his uncle Mike, who lived in New York, than he did of his father.

'Was Uncle Mike in the crash, too?' he asked Crystal.

'No.'

'Who else died?' Luke needed to know. 'The pilot?'

'No, sweetie. Your father was flying himself. He was alone, as far as we know. The helicopter came down over the ocean. Nobody saw it crash, but the coastguard found some wreckage. I'm sorry, honey. There was no chance of survivors. Jack's gone.'

'I have to go see Megan,' Luke told Crystal.

'We'll find out where she is,' Mom replied.

Luke got out his phone.

'Isn't it a little early . . . ?' Mom asked.

'If I know Megan, she won't have slept.'

No signal. You needed quad band for a US phone to work in the UK, Luke remembered, and he only had dual band. If Luke was going to stay in the UK for any length of time, Dad would have to get him a new phone.

And then it hit him. There was no Dad to get him a new phone. There was no Dad ever again.

They only had carry-on baggage so, once they'd cleared Customs, Luke and Crystal got on the Heathrow Express train to Paddington Station. Luke tried not to look at the other passengers' newspapers. Then he couldn't stop himself. He didn't know which to be hurt by most: the ones that had *Top Industrialist Killed In Copter Crash* as their main headline or the ones that led on the elections in Pakistan, demoting Dad to an inside page. It was weird, seeing Jack Kite's face on the front of so many newspapers. The USA had hundreds of billionaire businessmen, but in the UK, Jack Kite was a very big deal. According to Uncle Mike, Jack was probably the richest living Brit who'd made all his own money. *Was.* Luke was half English, but he had never felt less so than he did today, hurtling into London to attend the funeral of a father he hardly knew. He did know why the two of them had come so quickly. It was the same reason

11

Crystal got together with Jack in the first place. It was all about the money.

There was still an overnight sleeper from Edinburgh to London. Megan travelled on it alone. She couldn't fly, not after what had happened. If Grace hadn't been in hospital, she would have come too. She and Megan had been close since primary school. Dad had flown the two of them in his helicopter more times than Megan could remember. She hated leaving Grace behind.

Dad was a safe pilot. He never took unnecessary risks. How could he let this happen? She was only seventeen years old and she was an orphan. Stop being melodramatic, Megan told herself. You're old enough to drive, almost old enough to vote. You have an uncle and a half-brother. Dad will have left you well provided for. Don't feel sorry for yourself. Feel sorry for Dad. He was only forty. He had half his life to live.

Megan knew that she was in shock. The head had warned her, offered grief counselling. But all Megan wanted to do was get on the train and cry herself to sleep. Not that she had slept much.

Nearly there. She got out her mobile, which had been turned off since her bike ride with Grace. She hadn't wanted to talk to anyone. There would be plenty of time for that in days to come. Now, though, she didn't want to queue for a cab at Euston. There might be press waiting, photographers. She phoned Kite Industries' UK office and asked for Dad's PA, who should have just arrived at work.

'Ruth, this is Megan Kite. I'm on the Caledonia sleeper

and I'll be arriving at Euston in a few minutes. Can you send a driver?'

'Of course, Megan, I'm so sorry. We're all in pieces here. If there's anything—'

Megan interrupted. She wasn't ready for condolence conversations.

'I'm going to the Barbican flat, Ruth. I'll call Uncle Mike later to talk about arrangements. I know it's the middle of the night there.'

They went into a tunnel and Megan hung up. When reception returned, she saw that she had eleven messages and three missed calls. She scrolled through them. The first two missed calls had come just as she was going into her final exam. Both were from Dad. He would have wanted to wish her luck. She began to weep uncontrollably.

The driver could see how upset she was and kept quiet all the way. At the Barbican, Megan thanked him for carrying her bags to the lift. He gave a grunt of acknowledgement. Megan went up alone. Entry to the flat was via a swipe card. The previous night, in a rush, Megan hadn't been able to find it. That was OK, there was also a complicated key code. She had it written down on a note in her purse. It took her a couple of goes to punch it in, then the door swung open. She was home.

But it was Dad's home rather than hers. Megan hardly used her room here. When she wasn't at school, Megan was rarely in the flat for long. There were so many holidays to take and friends all over the world to visit. In London, she spent as much time at Grace's as she did here. But not this

13

time. Megan took her stuff through to the bedroom, then made a drink. Dad had been away. There was no milk in the fridge. Most of the food had passed its use-by date. In the last cupboard she looked in, Megan located some long-life milk and a single tea bag.

Dad's answerphone indicated that he had twenty-three new messages. Megan couldn't face her own messages, never mind his. The kettle boiled and she poured water into a mug, then sat down for a minute to let her tea brew. She gazed out of the wide, body-height windows at the cityscape below, but couldn't keep her eyes open. Next thing she knew it was hours later and something had woken her up. Then there was a scraping noise at the door.

Someone was trying to break in.

'I don't understand why we're here,' Luke had told his mom, two hours earlier.

'To show respect,' Crystal replied.

'But the funeral won't be for days yet.'

'You're family. And we need to establish that before the vultures start circling. Your father would have wanted you to have half of everything.'

'He never promised me that,' Luke said. 'He never promised me anything. Money's corrupting. I don't want it.'

'How do you think you'll pay to go to university, unless you have your father's money? Out of my allowance? With Jack gone, I don't even know if I'll keep getting an allowance!'

'I can work, or get a loan. Whatever.'

Crystal was only worried about herself, as usual. Jack Kite

had given her a generous allowance to cover Luke's upbringing. Not for herself. She had never lived with Jack, never mind married him. The way Dad told it, he came to the States and began travelling, setting up software franchises. He began with basic word-processing packages and educational games. He visited forty-eight states and his absences caused his marriage to Megan's mom to crumble. Jack met Crystal when she was working as a waitress in a classy New York steak house on one of those roads between Sixth and Seventh Avenue. She'd dropped out of college and was trying to make it as an actress. She'd taken a couple of classes but had not even made it to off-off-Broadway. There were some modelling jobs, but they weren't the kind of pictures you showed your only son.

Jack had dropped hints about what happened. They had a one-night stand and Crystal got pregnant. At which point, Jack told her that he was married. Not only that, but he was trying for a reconciliation with his wife. If Crystal wanted to keep the baby, he promised he would take his responsibilities seriously. But not too seriously.

Crystal was a good mom, except when she was hooked up with unsuitable guys, which was about half of the time. But Jack was barely a dad. He thought that by giving Crystal a steadily increasing allowance, he was doing right by Luke. Luke thought money was meaningless. Mike agreed with him, said that Dad's millions were just a 'way of keeping score'. But they impressed Crystal.

Luke and Crystal dumped their stuff in a cheap hotel in Bloomsbury, then took a cab to Kite Industries' headquarters. Outside, Sky News were preparing to do a live report. Seeing the cameras, Mom went bounding over to a guy in a baseball cap. She knew how to spot a producer. She looked like she was pimping Luke to do an interview. Luke wasn't having that. As the producer turned round, looking for a photogenic, bereaved son, Luke kept walking. He was sixteen now. No longer under his mom's thumb. Now that they were in London, there was only one place he wanted to go. He wasn't taking Mom there.

Luke found an ATM and checked his balance. There was a thousand dollars in his account that wasn't there yesterday. So Dad hadn't forgotten his birthday after all. He drew out a hundred pounds, then bought a one-day travel pass. He would have to buy a phone too, but that could wait. He was by a tube station. Goodge Street. He checked the tube map and worked out the route to his destination.

Behind him, there was no sign of Crystal. Mom never used subways. She would worry about where he was. Let her. She'd dragged him all the way here and threatened to humiliate or embarrass him. But now that Luke was in London, he had business of his own.

Three

The scraping noise ceased. Maybe Megan had dreamt it. She looked at her watch. Midday. A new noise began, faint but familiar. Somebody was typing numbers into the entry device.

Megan panicked and reached for her phone. There were burglars, she'd read, who targeted the homes of the newly dead, knowing they would be empty. This flat had high-tech security, but if the thieves thought the place was empty, they wouldn't worry about doing a smash-and-grab before the police came.

Was there an alarm button? Megan was pretty sure the complex had its own security guards. They would be quicker than dialling the police. Trembling, sweating, she hurried to the door, scared that at any moment it would be smashed open. Yes, there was a red button on the security panel. There was also a fish-eye security lens. Megan leant over and looked through. Then she let out a deep breath and unlocked the door.

Her half-brother took a step back, looking dazed.

'I knocked a couple of times but there was no response.'

'I was asleep. Did you really think you could break in?'

'I tried the old credit-card-down-the-side-of-the-lock

trick. No luck. I've been desperately guessing numbers for the last minute. I tried using your cell number.'

'You could have rung me,' Megan said, closing the door behind him. 'That would have woken me up.'

'My phone doesn't work here.'

'Never mind.' She rattled off the security number, then they gave each other an awkward half hug.

Luke broke the hug first. 'Have you heard from Uncle Mike?'

Megan shook her head. 'I was going to ring him. What time is it?'

'Over there? Only seven a.m.'

'Maybe I should call now, see what I should be doing.'

'OK,' Luke said.

Megan tapped her uncle's personal number into the speed dial on her phone. It went straight to answering service.

'I'll try Kite Industries.'

She was put through to Mike's PA.

'Mr Kite is on a plane to the UK to arrange your father's funeral. I believe he arrives in three hours' time. May I offer my condolences? All of us here are deeply—'

'Thank you,' Megan interrupted. 'Thank you. It's a very difficult time. I'll call my uncle again later.'

She looked at her phone, which she'd left on silent. There were a bunch more messages, but only one she wanted to listen to. Grace. She left it, rather than be rude to Luke. She hated it when people looked at their phones, ignoring friends who'd come to see them. And Luke was more than a friend.

'Some sixteenth birthday present, huh?' she said.

Luke gave a hopeless shrug and pointed at the

flashing answerphone. 'Think we should listen to some of those messages?'

'I don't know. I was going to ask Mike. What do you think?'

'I think it's up to us. We're his heirs, right?'

'I suppose. But I don't want to be . . . intrusive, you know what I mean?'

'This is Dad we're talking about. He worked so hard he didn't have time for a private life.'

'I guess you're right. Let's get them out of the way.'

Luke pressed 'play'. Most of the messages did sound like business. Seven were about meetings. One was from a woman with a French accent.

'*Cherie*? I thought you would be here by now. I tried your mobile but you have no signal. Have I got the day wrong?'

This message was from the day before. Luke and Megan looked at each other. This was the woman who their father was flying to meet. There was one more call from the same number, no message. Then the calls from journalists began.

'I was hoping you could call me back and give me a comment for our news story. I am sorry for your tragic loss.'

They deleted all of these. Then the phone rang. Impulsively, Megan answered it, hoping for Uncle Mike, even though she knew he was in the air.

'Megan? This is Crystal, Luke's mom. Is he there?'

No condolences, just her brittle Brooklyn accent.

'Sure. I'll hand him over.'

Megan watched as her brother was berated by his mother.

'I didn't want to talk to the media,' he said twice. 'That's why I left. No, don't come here.' He put the phone down for a moment. 'Is there food?' he asked Megan. She shook her head. 'No, there isn't. OK, if you insist.' He hung up.

'What was all that about?' Megan asked, careful not to sound critical. Crystal *was* Luke's mother, even if Dad used to call her a 'hateful harridan'. There must be some good in her.

'I dumped Mom outside the Kite Industry offices. She was talking to the media and I didn't want anything to do with it.'

'Good for you.'

'She's coming over with some food.'

'Oh. OK.'

If Megan needed to eat, she could phone for a take-away, but never mind. Maybe Crystal meant well.

'Did she talk to anyone at the office?'

'It sounds like they wouldn't give her the time of day.'

And why should they? Megan thought.

'Have you called Grandma?'

She shook her head and grimaced.

'Yeah, I know what you mean.'

Dad's mother was in a nursing home and had Alzheimer's. What was the point in telling her that her eldest son was gone? She would soon forget, then Megan or Luke or Mike would have to remind her, every time they visited. Megan's maternal grandparents were both long gone. That left their uncle.

'Let's wait for Mike,' she said. 'I don't want to talk to anyone until I've seen him.'

They hadn't seen each other for months but now, exhausted and upset, each found they had nothing to say.

'Should I turn on the TV?' Luke asked.

'You might as well.'

The screen showed wreckage from Dad's helicopter, floating in the North Sea.

'*Jack Kite was the founder, chairperson and majority shareholder of Kite Industries, the world's second biggest software company. The billionaire businessman was returning from a race meeting in Cork when, it is believed, he had engine problems. Air traffic control received a distress signal but were unable to contact Jack Kite. By the time coastguards reached the area, this debris was all that remained.*'

There was a capsule biography of Luke and Megan's father, followed by a brief interview with Mike Kite, snatched in the middle of the night, as he arrived at JFK to catch a plane to the UK.

'I haven't fully taken it in yet. It's a tragedy. I have no further comment at this time,' Mike said.

'How come you and your mom were able to get here quicker than Uncle Mike?' Megan asked.

'I dunno,' Luke said. 'Maybe Mike had things to do first.'

On the TV screen, Sky had found a couple of Dad's 'friends' to interview. Neither were people Dad had mentioned to Megan. When the piece was over, the news cycle started again, updating every fifteen minutes. They watched the report on Dad's death twice. There was no new information. Luke began to look around the flat, with its ultra-modern furniture and antique paintings. Some of them – Megan wasn't sure which – were awfully valuable. Dad said that modern art was over-priced because rich buyers liked to meet the artists. But he wasn't interested in living artists. He liked masterpieces that he knew would last. And he liked a bargain.

'When were you last here?' Megan asked Luke.

'I've only stayed here once. A couple of years ago. Dad gave me the code to get in and I wrote it down, but I didn't know I was coming, so I forgot to bring it with me.'

Should she ask him to stay with her? Megan wondered. She would be happy to have Luke around, but there was also his mum. She'd never met Crystal, unless you counted seeing her fleetingly when Dad collected Luke for their occasional holidays together. But she'd built her up in her mind as an ogre, the woman who tried to steal Dad from Mum. Oh, she knew Dad was no saint, but it took two—

There was a loud knock on the door.

'That sounds like Mom,' Luke called. 'I'll let her in.'

The woman who walked into the living room, carrying two Harrods bags, looked impossibly young. How old was Crystal when she'd had Luke? Twelve? She could be an MTV presenter, with hair so blonde it was nearly white and pert, perfect breasts. She put down the bags, then hurried over to Megan and hugged her. Luke's mother smelled of vanilla.

'I'm so sorry, sweetie. Your dad was such a great man.'

'Thank you.' Megan broke away from the hug and turned off the TV. Crystal didn't know Megan and she hated Jack Kite. Megan hated hypocrites.

'What a lovely place,' Crystal said. 'Where's the kitchen? I'm going to make you two some lunch.'

'It's the next room.' Megan pointed. She was about to say that she wasn't hungry. Then she decided that it was a good idea to give Crystal something to do.

Crystal took her time. The food, when it came, was all pre-prepared. Little spinach pies. A bulgar wheat salad with a piquant sauce. Onion bread. Slivers of smoked duck. Megan was surprised to find herself wolfing it down. Luke ate hungrily too, though he turned his nose up at the bulgar wheat.

'You know I won't touch healthy crap like this!'

'Just because it's good for you doesn't mean it tastes awful,' said Crystal. She herself picked at the food. It was like if she chewed every mouthful less than a hundred times it would instantly sprout into a bump on her perfectly flat tummy. Then she pushed her plate aside and, while the siblings ate, tried to make conversation, asking about school, friends, holidays. At another time, such talk might have been OK. It took ten minutes for Crystal to turn to the subject that Megan had been expecting her to raise ever since she showed up.

'Do you know if your father made a will?'

'I'm sure he did. After my mum died, you know . . .'

'Oh, you poor child. You're an orphan now. You know, if you ever need anything from me, anything at all.'

Megan nodded and half smiled as though she were seriously considering this generous offer.

'And where would he keep this will, do you know?'

'Not here,' Megan said. 'At the family lawyers', I suppose.'

'And they are?'

To Megan's relief, the phone rang. She beat Luke to it.

'Megan, darling, how are you holding up?'

'It's all so awful, Mike. I don't know what to do.'

23

'Are you in Jack's flat on your own?'

'Luke and his mother are here.'

'I expect that Crystal's the last person you need to see right now.'

'Kinda.'

'Best if I talk to you alone. OK if I get rid of them?'

'How . . . ?'

'Just let me talk to Crystal. I know how to deal with her.'

Megan handed the phone to Luke's mother then sat down. She was feeling awfully tired.

'You OK?' Luke asked.

'I'm really, really knackered,' she said.

'*Knackered*! Like they do to horses, right? You Brits use some weird words.'

Crystal came off the phone. 'Sweetie, we need to go.'

'But I want to hang with Megan!'

'Look how tired she is. Mike's coming over. We should go.'

Four

'It was nice of you to bring lunch, Crystal,' Megan said.

'I'd like to get to know you better,' Crystal said, in a fake tone that made Luke squirm.

'Come on, Mom,' Luke said.

'Of course. We'll get going.' Crystal gave Luke a sharp look. He gave his sister a hug.

'Come and see me again,' she murmured in his ear.

'Sure,' he said quietly, then added, in his normal voice, 'I'll call you when I've got a working cell phone.'

'Great.'

'Here,' Crystal said, putting a card on the low, glass, living-room table. 'This has our hotel address and number on it.'

'Thank you,' Megan said. 'Thank you so much.'

She ushered them out.

'I think she could have been a little more gracious, considering that we've just flown all the way over here,' Crystal said, as they waited for the elevator.

'We've just lost our dad,' Luke reminded her. 'Nothing's normal.'

'Do you have a key for this place?'

'No, but there's a security code I can use. Megan told me

25

the number, but I've forgotten it already.'

'I see.' There was an awkward pause as they went down eight floors, then Mom perked up. 'While we're in London, with nothing better to do, we should do some tourist things. How far are we from Tate Modern?'

'Not too far.' Luke knew how to get there, though he had no desire to visit an art gallery the day after his dad had died. He suggested taking the tube, but Crystal wouldn't hear of it. They had to go everywhere in the 'cute' black cabs. What they were doing for money, Luke didn't like to ask.

The Tate was impressive. It opened into a massive hall, which was filled by a sculpture that resembled a gigantic octopus, its tentacles reaching up to the galleries on different floors, each one acting as a flume that descended into a vast cushioned area at the base of the octopus. On any other day, Luke might have stood in line to go down one of the tentacles.

'They call this place the Turbine Hall,' Crystal said. 'Any idea what that means?'

'Didn't it used to be some kind of power station?'

'Maybe it used to have those wind turbines in here?'

How would the turbines catch the wind if they were inside? Luke thought but didn't ask. His mother was prone to asking stupid questions as a means of making conversation. Also, it suited her to make people think that she was less smart than she really was. Crystal knew that Luke knew better, but playing the ditsy blonde was still second nature to her.

'Coming?'

'Not today.'

Luke watched as Crystal lined up, then slid down the flume like a nervous nine-year-old, screaming as she sped up.

When she landed, Mom's pink Gucci bag went flying off the soft mattresses onto the hard floor. Luke collected it. Crystal spilled her stuff out onto the marble.

'No! My phone's been dinted.'

'It's hardly noticeable,' Luke said. 'Question is, does it still work?'

Crystal switched it on. 'Will I be able to tell? You said our phones don't work here.'

'Mine doesn't. Yours might.'

And, of course, it turned out that Mom's phone was not only flume-proof but also got a signal in the UK. Mom listened to her messages. Her face seemed to pale beneath the make-up.

'What is it?' Luke asked, but Mom ignored him, concentrating on whatever was at the other end. When she hung up, she seemed to have aged ten years.

'What is it?' Luke repeated.

'There's been a terrible accident, the police say. Some kind of gas explosion. Our home, everything inside, it's all been completely destroyed!'

Uncle Mike made Megan a mug of strong coffee.

'You'll need this,' he said. 'We've got a lot to talk about.'

Just seeing him upset Megan. Mike looked so much like his brother. He was Dad with a bald patch in his brown hair, a slight beer belly and a squarer jaw.

'Crystal wanted to know about Dad's will,' Megan told him.

'Figures. Generally, the solicitor won't sanction a will reading until after the funeral, that's the form. But we can't have a proper funeral until they recover a body. I'm sorry to have to tell you this but, given that the helicopter exploded, it's unlikely the authorities will recover a recognizable body.'

'Then what about the funeral?'

'That'll have to wait until the authorities declare Jack dead. That shouldn't take too long. We know he was flying the 'copter. There'll be DNA traces and so on. But it may take a while. I think we should hold a memorial service first. I'll ask the solicitor about the will. If that's OK with you.'

'Fine, thanks.' Megan suddenly felt very tired. 'Was there something else you needed to talk to me about?'

'There is. I know that all you want to do is grieve. Me too, but I have to be concerned with Kite Industries. When a CEO dies suddenly, investors start to panic. Jack has always been perceived as the main force behind the company, even after it went public, even after I took over running the US wing. Since the stock exchanges opened, our share price has been in free fall. So I need to put on a strong front. We're about to make an announcement that I'm taking over as CEO, that it's business as usual and your father's death won't affect any of Kite Industries' core activities. I wanted you to be informed first.'

'Thanks,' Megan said. 'I appreciate . . .'

'Megan, are you OK?'

'I just feel very tired all of a sudden. I slept earlier but I feel . . . weird. I think I need to lie down.'

'I'll help you.'

For the first time since she was a toddler, her uncle put her to bed.

When they got back to the hotel, Luke rang Megan to see how she was. He wanted to tell her about the explosion as well. It was an accident, Mom said, but it was also a big coincidence. There was no reply on Megan's cell or on Dad's home phone. Luke left messages on both. Crystal turned on the rolling news channel. There was Uncle Mike, coming out of the Kite Industries headquarters.

'*The Kite family are deeply affected by this tragic loss. But we want our investors and our customers to know that this will have no effect on Kite Industries' core activities. The board has just met. I have its full support and, of course, that of the Kite family, in taking over as acting CEO until further notice.*'

'Full support?' Crystal said. 'I didn't hear Mike ask you whether you wanted him in charge.'

Luke shrugged. He got on well with Uncle Mike. They went out to eat from time to time, took in a movie or a ball game. Mike was single – or at least he always lived alone – and had a cool apartment on the Upper West Side.

'If he'd asked, I'd've said yes. Who else could take charge? Anyway, it's a public company. It's not like Kite Industries was Dad's private fiefdom. The board's what counts. He probably told Megan out of politeness.'

'But he could have—'

'Sssh, I'm trying to listen. Something's happening.'

Mike was saying something boring about financial figures. A reporter from the BBC had begun to shout over him.

'Mr Kite, Mr Kite! We're getting fresh reports in that a terrorist group are claiming responsibility for your brother's death. The group, the ACW, say that your brother's helicopter was shot down because Kite Industries provides software essential for the smart use of chemical warfare. They're saying . . .' He hesitated. 'I'm sorry, this is just coming in over my headphones. They're saying that if Kite Industries doesn't withdraw from this kind of programming, none of your employees will be safe, including yourself. How do you respond?'

Mike sounded flustered. 'Whenever somebody powerful dies in an unexplained manner, you have cranks wanting to claim responsibility. I won't dignify this nonsense by responding to it further.'

The words were strong but his face told a different story. Mike Kite turned his back on the cameras and hurried into the Kite Industries building.

Five

Megan stirred uneasily. How long had she been asleep? Her side was stiff and her body ached. Her head felt fuzzy. She remembered vivid, terrifying dreams involving her mother and father. When she tried to recall what happened in them, the images slipped away. Her arms were raw, sore, where someone seemed to have scratched her. Or maybe she had scratched herself.

Megan tried to move and nothing happened. Where was she? It felt like her room in the flat. The blinds were drawn and she couldn't tell if it was night or day. Somebody or something had made a noise, waking her up. That was it. Somebody was ringing the doorbell. She tried to drag herself out of bed, but could barely move. Then she heard the door open.

Who had the code to get in? Uncle Mike, presumably. And Luke, but he hadn't written it down . . . Someone called her name. Megan tried to reply but her voice was weak, empty. The bedroom door opened. Megan wanted to lift herself up to see who it was, only she didn't have the strength. She could see a shadow crossing the room, but had no sense of who it was. If she didn't feel so ill, she would be scared.

The blinds were pulled open and light flooded in. Her brother was standing in front of the window. He wore the same clothes as when he'd come before, ripped jeans and a grey, cotton jacket.

'Megan! I didn't know you were here. I've been calling and ringing the doorbell. Eventually I managed to guess the code.'

'I've been really tired and . . . I dunno, ill I think. I don't know what's wrong with me.'

Luke came over, felt her forehead. 'Have you come in contact with anyone odd?'

'Dunno. I've been in bed for ages. What do you mean, anyone odd?'

'I'm talking about the terrorism claims on the TV. They have all kinds of high-tech poisons these days.'

'What terrorism claims?' Megan asked. 'I have no idea what you're talking about.'

Now it was Luke's turn to look confused. 'How long have you been sick?'

'I have no idea. I started feeling rough about an hour after you left yesterday. Uncle Mike was here. What time is it now?'

Luke sat down on the edge of the bed. 'Megan, that wasn't yesterday. That was three days ago.'

Could she really have been ill for so long? Megan struggled to get the words out. 'I guess you better call a doctor.'

'I don't think so,' Luke said. 'I don't think you're safe here.'

'Then call Uncle Mike!'

'I'm pretty sure he's busy at the moment,' Luke told her.

'I'll explain later. Are you well enough to get up? If I can get you downstairs and into a taxi, we can get you to a hospital.'

'I might be able to dress with your help,' Megan said. 'But I don't understand. Why wouldn't I be safe?'

'There's been all sorts of stuff in the papers these last three days. A terrorist group called the ACW has claimed responsibility for Dad's death. They say Kite Industries coded software that had been used to detonate incredibly toxic chemical weapons. They say they shot down Dad's helicopter. And they made it clear that anyone with strong connections to Kite Industries is a legitimate target. That means me and you.'

'I . . . I . . .' Megan gagged. Then she found herself being sick, all over the off-white pile carpet. Puking, instead of making her feel gross, actually made her feel a little better. She was able to reach for the glass of stale water on the bedside table.

'What are we going to do?' she asked her brother.

'I really think I should get you out of here,' Luke said. He used tissues to wipe the vomit from the carpet, without much success. Then he helped her clean up, dress and get some stuff together. Her brother was acting as though it wasn't safe to return. Megan remembered reading about Russians poisoning each other with tiny particles of heavy metals. It would have been easy for somebody to sneak something toxic into Dad's flat before she arrived. Something radioactive. It needn't even have been left for her. If the terrorist story were true, the poison might have been meant for Dad, a back-up plan in case shooting him down didn't work. Only, in that case, why wasn't she dead?

Terrorists who targeted a software company? It seemed far-fetched. But Dad was a very good helicopter pilot, and he was dead. Luke propped up her arm so that she could stagger into the kitchen. The food wrappers from Harrods were still on the counter. While Luke phoned for a cab, she poured herself a glass of water from the tap.

'Anything else you need from here?' Luke asked. 'It might not be safe to come back.'

Had things really become so dangerous, so quickly? A lot of her stuff was still in Scotland. She instructed Luke to pack some underwear and a USB stick with all her most important data backed up. It felt like they were going on the run. But on the run from what?

'Come on,' Luke said. 'Let's go.'

He helped her out of the flat and used the code to lock it behind them. Now that she was moving, her strength was returning a little.

'Why did you come round?' she asked her brother. 'Was it because you were worried about me, or is there another reason?'

'It's the same reason Uncle Mike's busy,' Luke explained. 'We're supposed to be at the reading of Dad's will. But I think our first priority is to get you to a hospital.'

Six

Luke hailed a taxi and bundled Megan into the back seat.

'Maybe I ought to phone Uncle Mike,' she said.

'His phone will be turned off.'

'I don't understand why he hasn't contacted me.'

Luke tried to explain. 'Mike's keeping his head down. There's a lot of strange stuff going on at the moment. One of the papers claims it was Uncle Mike who did the business with the government that makes the chemical weapons. So he could be the ACW terrorists' next target.'

'ACW. "Against Chemical Weapons"?'

'I think so.' Luke got out his new phone, a cheap pay-as-you-go, and punched in Crystal's number. His mother answered on the second ring.

'Well?'

'Megan can't get to the will reading. She's sick. I need to look after her. Can you go on our behalf?'

'I suppose. Let me speak to her for a moment.'

Luke handed over the phone. Megan looked uncomfortable. Probably she didn't like Crystal much. Luke had no choice about loving her. She was his mother. If she weren't, he wasn't sure that he'd even like her.

'Yeah. OK. Thanks.' Megan handed the phone back.

'Where are you?' Crystal asked Luke.

'It doesn't matter. I'll see you back at the hotel.'

He hung up. The taxi pulled in to Casualty. It was a bleak building, but no shabbier than the public health outfits in Brooklyn. At Reception, a nurse took Megan's information and told her that she shouldn't have to wait more than an hour. 'Unless something big comes in.'

'You're rich,' Luke said, as they sat down to wait in a hard plastic chair. 'There must be somewhere private you could go.'

'Private healthcare's no good for emergencies,' Megan said. 'Don't worry. I'll be fine. I'm already feeling a little better.'

'Perhaps if we told them you might have been poisoned.'

'Then somebody would overhear and call the media.'

Megan got out her phone and began to check her messages. To distract himself, Luke watched the TV blaring away in the corner of the room. A home makeover show was replaced by the *News at One*. The third story was one Luke had hoped Megan wouldn't see. Too late. She was looking up.

'*A memorial service was held this morning for Jack Kite, the leading industrialist who was killed in a helicopter crash last week. Media were not allowed into the service at St Paul's Cathedral because of terrorist threats made against members of the Kite family. Participants who spoke to the BBC described the service as "emotional, but marked by anger". A funeral cannot be held until Mr Kite's remains have been identified and a formal inquest has taken place. Amongst the mourners were . . .*'

The newsreader gave a litany of politicians, business

leaders and celebrities. The picture showed floral tributes from President Obama and Bill Gates. Megan began to cry.

'I only just heard the phone message about the service. How could I not be there? What will people think?'

'That you were too sick or too upset. It's what I thought. That's why I came here as soon as the service was over.'

'I can't believe he's gone, Luke.'

He held her as she cried. Then a doctor came. Luke, since he was family, was allowed to be with Megan while they did tests. But there were no quick answers. A blood test was followed by a saliva test. The results could take hours, the specialist said.

Luke's phone rang. It would be Crystal, reporting back on the will reading. A nurse waved at him and pointed at the 'no mobile phones to be turned on' sign. Luke pressed 'ignore' and turned his phone off. He wasn't expecting much from the will and Megan was too out of it to care about anything at the moment. He went outside to return his mother's call.

'Where are you? I've been trying to find you since I left the solicitor's!' Crystal screeched.

'I'm outside the hospital. Like I told you, Megan's sick.'

'Which hospital? I need to know!'

'It doesn't matter which hospital,' Luke said. He didn't want his mother coming here. 'What happened at the will reading?'

'There was nothing for me,' Crystal moaned.

What was she expecting? Luke wondered. A meal ticket for life? 'What about me?' he ventured.

'There was nothing for you either, hon. At least, not yet.'

'What do you mean, *not yet*?'

'You have your trust.'

'Trust? I don't know anything about a trust.'

'Your father set up a trust fund just after you were born, to mature when you were eighteen. It's to pay for college fees, with a chunk left over.'

'So that stuff the other day about you not being able to put me through college was crap.'

'I never told you because I didn't believe he meant the rest of what he said. He said that after that you were on your own. I thought that he should leave you half of everything. I'm sorry.'

'It's as much as I could've expected,' Luke said. 'I don't believe in inherited wealth anyway. You should make your own way in the world.'

'That was what your father felt.'

'How about Megan? What did he leave her?'

'There are some charitable donations, and Mike gets some stock and a few personal items, but, basically, on her eighteenth birthday, Megan inherits everything.'

'I see.' Luke said. Hard not to feel resentful. Megan was the first born, the wanted child, the light of Jack's life. Luke was merely his only son. Boys should make their own way in the world. Girls needed to be protected. He kicked the hospital's brick wall.

'Maybe it's time to go home,' Crystal said.

'Terrorists just blew up our home.'

'We don't know that. The police say it was probably a fault with the gas line. You're safer in the US than you are here.'

'I want to be around for Megan. Why would I be threatened?'

'You were at the memorial service. They showed your picture on TV. You're a target, Luke.'

'Then maybe I'd better keep a low profile and not fly anywhere for a while.'

'I want you to come home with me tomorrow.'

'I'll think about it. But right now I want to find out how Megan is.'

When he returned to Casualty, his sister was still sleeping. Luke spoke to the doctor in charge of her case.

'It's clear that her body has gone through some kind of intense trauma.'

'You think she was poisoned?'

'Or exposed to some kind of radiation, yes. Have you spoken to the police?'

'Not yet. I thought that would be better coming from her.'

'I see. Where has she been for the last few days?'

'At a flat in the Barbican. Before that, on a train, and at school in Scotland.'

The doctor was thoughtful. 'You'd better give me the Barbican address and the name of the school. Also, the train if you know it. We could be talking about finding traces of radiation poisoning. When did she last eat?'

'Just over three days ago. I was there. The food was from Harrods, for crying out loud! I shared it with her.'

'OK, stick around. We should have the rest of the test results back within a couple of hours.'

Seven

The doctor told Megan that she was well enough to leave, but that she should wait for the police.

'Initial tests suggest that you came into contact with 3-Quinuclidinyl benzilate, which is an incapacitating agent. The Iraqis called this gas Agent 15. Europeans call it BZ. It's never been used in this country, so our experience is limited and our results are inconclusive. We'll do further tests on the samples.'

'Is there an antidote?' Megan asked.

'Yes. Physostigmine. But BZ's not fatal and you're over the worst. It's an unusual case. Can you think of any way you could have come into contact with it?'

'How would I know?'

'Good question. The stuff's odourless and tasteless, and it can take anything from half an hour to thirty-six hours to take effect. The average is two hours and the effects tend to last for two days. There are no long-term effects, you'll be pleased to know. We have to inform the security services of your exposure to it and I'll need to book you some follow-up tests.'

'Of course.' Megan agreed to the dates suggested. She had no plans to get in the way. She had no plans whatsoever.

Luke was waiting in a cab by the exit. They crossed

London in streams of vivid sunlight. It was late afternoon and the city seemed loose, relaxed and ready for play. The opposite of how Megan felt. She told Luke everything the doctor said.

'Shouldn't we go straight to the police?'

'I think I should see Uncle Mike before I go to the police. If I was attacked by terrorists, he needs to know first.'

'Uncle Mike's line was that the terrorists were publicity seekers and Dad's death was an accident. But this should change his mind.'

When they got to Kite Industries, the atmosphere was strained. Security was high. Megan had to show her ID three times and each time she had to talk Luke in with her, as he wasn't on the list of authorized visitors. She had to leave her brother in a reception area before she was allowed in to what had been her father's office. Dad's PA looked embarrassed when she saw Megan walk in.

'My dear, I'm so sorry. We've all been in terrible shock here. I wanted to call you, but it's been such a turbulent time.'

'That's OK,' Megan told Ruth. She had learned from Dad that there was work and there was the personal but it was better not to mix the two. Employees could be friendly at work, but they were not your friends.

'Were you too upset to attend the service this morning?'

'No, I was taken ill.'

Before the PA could express concern, Megan asked, 'Can I see my Uncle Mike? I gather he's in charge at the moment.'

'Mr Kite has flown back to the US.'

Without me? Megan nearly said. But she was her own person, even if she felt alone and very vulnerable. Mike didn't know about the poison gas, if that was what it was. She might need him, but she had finished school and he had a company to run. Uncle Mike could hardly be expected to become her guardian. She turned eighteen in three months and would have no need for one. Only, where was she meant to go?

'Did my uncle arrange protection for me?' she asked Ruth.

'Yes. He asked Tom Morris, our head of security, to organize it. You were left a message about it.'

'OK.' Megan was beginning to feel tired again. She didn't want to be assertive. She didn't want to offend anyone. Maybe Uncle Mike thought she hadn't been returning his calls, that she was angry with him for some reason. She didn't feel like tracking down Tom Morris. She wanted to be with friends, but now that school was over, they were scattered around the world. Except one. And she owed her a visit.

'I need to travel,' she told the PA, 'and I can't risk using any kind of public transport again. Can you have a helicopter ready in fifteen minutes?'

'A helicopter? After . . .'

She didn't need to finish the sentence. But Megan had been flying in helicopters all her life. She had no intention of stopping. They were too convenient. And she needed to get in one soon, before flying in one again became a big deal.

'Nobody knows I'm here. They're hardly going to shoot me down, if that's what really happened to my father.'

'Of course.' Megan watched as the PA made the phone call.

42

'And tell Tom I'll be gone overnight, but I want to see him on my return.'

'I'll do that,' the PA said.

'OK. I'm going to have a word with my brother before I go.'

She joined Luke in Reception and told him where she was going. 'You can come with me if you want.'

'No. Three's a crowd. You want to be with your friend, I understand. And Mom's anxious to get back to the States. She'll feel safer there, even if we haven't got anywhere to live. Why don't you come?'

'Maybe I will. I'm meant to be starting work in an African village, miles from anywhere, in a couple of weeks.'

'You're rich now, or you will be. You can give away enough money to help a hundred villages.'

'What do you mean?'

'My mom told me about Dad's will. When you turn eighteen, you get nearly everything. Mike gets some stock. I have a trust fund.'

'I see.' Megan thought for a moment. 'And what happens if I don't make it to eighteen?'

'I didn't ask.'

'Why don't you get half? Is your trust fund huge? Did Dad discuss it with you?'

Luke shrugged. 'I'm not all that interested in money, Megan. Maybe Dad knew that.'

'Are you saying that I am?'

'No, no,' Luke insisted, none too convincingly. It was true, Megan liked being rich. She couldn't imagine life any other way. But she'd give up everything to have her dad back.

Eight

SCOTLAND

During the hot, noisy, uncomfortable flight to Scotland, Megan tried to make sense of things. First, there was Dad's will. She was about to be very rich. But so what? She had always been rich. Owning all of Dad's stock in Kite Industries would be a lot of hassle. At least Uncle Mike would be able to help her.

Then there was the terrorism claim. She couldn't get her head round that. Best to request a briefing with Tom Morris when she returned. Megan didn't want the company to give in to threats, but she didn't want to be involved in chemical or biological weapons either. She'd ask for details of the chemical weapons software the ACW were complaining about. Chances were the 'terrorists' were fakes, pathetic attention seekers.

Which left the poisoning. Had somebody gassed her to scare the company, to back up the terrorism claims? If they'd wanted to kill her, they could have done. Or did somebody just want to get Megan out of the way for a couple of days? It made no sense. She should have gone to the police like the doctor wanted her to. But she would see Tom Morris first.

The pilot leaned back and shouted over the harsh engine noise. 'I'll need to book a helipad, ma'am.'

'No, you won't. I'll tell you where to land. You won't need to reserve it at this time of day,' Megan told him.

The other thing on her mind was Luke. Was it fair that she should get all the money and he only got enough to live on while he was at university? Maybe she should give him some. Maybe she should give him half. But that would be to disrespect her father's wishes. Dad always had good reasons. She'd discuss what to do with Uncle Mike.

Brunts School had a helipad behind the gym. As the helicopter descended, stern-faced security guards hurried over. Recognizing Megan, they relaxed. When she got out, they didn't give her any bother for not alerting the school to her arrival. Megan had always felt golden here, liked for herself more than for her money. Everyone here had money. Except the staff, obviously. It was good to be back.

Around them, the school day was ending. Only the final year students had left. The rest of the school didn't break up for summer until next month.

'I need to see the Head,' Megan told the Head of Security. Behind him, students left the gym. Nobody gawped. They were used to helicopters coming and going, especially at weekends. Rich parents would visit, often whisking their children away for holidays. Megan had often given Grace a lift.

Mrs Duncan met Megan in her study. As was her way, she got straight to the point.

'Is it true what the news said about your father?'

'I don't know. I don't know very much, except that

45

somebody tried to run me over, then they tried to poison me.'

Megan explained what had happened in London. 'I've come to pack up my stuff and to see Grace.'

'Of course.' The Head used her kindest voice. 'You must feel free to stay here, if this is a place you feel safe.'

'I've finished school.'

'Your father paid the fees until the end of term. You're welcome at Brunts for as long as you like. Our security is second to none. That's what your father paid for. Let us help.'

'Thanks,' Megan said. It was true, she would feel very safe here. But returning to school, just days after she'd finished for good? It would feel weird.

'You're not eighteen yet, Megan. We still have a duty of care to you. Why don't you stay the night, after you've seen Grace? I'm sure we can accommodate your pilot, too.'

'Thanks,' Megan replied. 'That would be good.'

'And I'll see if I can arrange for the police to put your mind at rest over the accident.'

'OK.'

'Good. I'll get my driver to take you over to see Grace in half an hour or so. Visiting begins at six-thirty.'

'I'm very grateful,' Megan said.

'Nonsense. That's what we're here for.'

Megan went to her room, the one she used to share with Grace. Nothing had changed. Like her, Grace had not had an opportunity to remove her stuff. From the rooms on either side came familiar sounds: gossip, laughter, music with strong beats, girls getting ready to begin their evening. But the girls who Megan had spent the last seven years with were gone for good. This large room felt both comforting and lonely.

Important to keep moving. She mustn't fall asleep again and miss seeing Grace. Megan began to take clothes out of her wardrobe. How much to pack? She didn't want to take all her stuff back to the Barbican flat. Maybe she'd go and stay with Uncle Mike in New York. If she filled her bag with enough clothes to last her a fortnight, that should see her through. Things were bound to be sorted out by then.

She was very tired though. How could she talk to Grace when she was so exhausted? Maybe if she rested for a few minutes. The Head would come and find her, so there was no chance of Megan missing visiting hours. A short sleep should revive her. A power nap, that was what Dad used to call it.

What woke her wasn't the Head, but the sound of a helicopter. The sound was getting further away, not nearer. That meant it was Megan's helicopter, leaving. She hadn't given permission for it to leave! Megan turned on the light and looked at her watch. Eleven! No wonder it was so quiet. Most girls were asleep by now. You weren't allowed to make noise after ten. Where was the Head? What was going on?

Then she spotted the note that someone had pushed under the door.

NEW YORK

The rooms in the Washington Square Hotel were on the small side but you couldn't fault the location. They overlooked the famous park, which was in the process of being renovated. The hotel had its own café in the basement where Luke could have breakfast. None of his friends were nearby, but most of them were on the move at this time of year anyhow. All of his possessions were gone. The only things he owned were the clothes he stood up in, two phones, and a twelve-gear bike.

'Once we've got somewhere to live, you can replace everything on the insurance,' Crystal said. 'There's no point in cluttering our lives up until then.'

'Sure, but why are we looking in Greenwich Village?' Luke asked. 'They say even millionaires can't afford places here.'

'We're not looking to buy, we're going to rent. It's time to be back in Manhattan, nearer the heart of things.'

'I prefer Brooklyn. It's home.'

'NYU is based all over this district. You might want to stick around and study here too.'

The idea of living with his mom while at college – if he got good enough grades to go – was sick, Luke thought. But he kept his mouth shut. He wondered if there was a man involved. Whenever they looked at moving apartments, there was usually a guy at the back of it all. Crystal tended to attract scumbags. Both the guys she'd lived with in Brooklyn had let her down badly.

'You ready?'

'I guess.'

The apartment viewings started at six. Luke was still on UK time, and by the time they left the first, a cramped brownstone, his body was telling him it was midnight. Luke thought about his sister. He felt bad about leaving Megan behind. Where was she now? With their uncle, presumably.

The third place they looked at was a two-bedroom apartment just off Sixth Avenue, with a view of the Christopher Street Park. There was no elevator, but there was a secure area in the lobby for him to stow his bike. The rooms were a good size, with unusually big windows. The previous occupant was a lawyer. He had left behind a built-in TV screen that took up a living-room wall, along with, much to Crystal's liking, a jacuzzi.

The apartment was crowded with potential tenants, well-dressed city types in their thirties and forties. The realtor kept telling everyone that the listed rent was only a guide price.

'The owners – let's put it this way – aren't expecting any offers that come in lower than the asking price.'

'I want it,' Crystal told her son.

'We'll never get it,' Luke told her. 'Look at these people. Some of them are seriously loaded.'

'Pah!' Crystal said. 'Watch me.'

Huddled in a corner by a tall window, Mom made a phone call. While Crystal spoke, new viewers kept arriving. Luke wasn't sure how comfortable this apartment was, with its easy-to-scratch wooden floors and high ceilings. This wasn't up to him, though. Once Crystal made up her mind about something, that was it.

When the call was over, Crystal returned to Luke. She was wearing one of her secretive smiles, the kind she gave him when he spotted her shoplifting.

'There's not a lot of storage space,' Luke pointed out.

'We haven't got a lot of stuff, remember? Or did you plan

to rebuy every bit of junk that you lost in the fire?'

'I . . . dunno.' Luke had lost his sneaker collection and hundreds of comic books, including some complete runs that were quite rare. Then there were his clothes and his computer stuff. Not to mention all the junk from his childhood that had been stuffed in the attic. Maybe Crystal was right, a clean start was what they needed. And the apartment *was* pretty cool.

The realtor's phone rang. Luke watched the woman's face as she took the call. What was that look? Daunted? Impressed? Intimidated? A moment later, it was gone, replaced by the standard measured Manhattan smile. She clapped her hands.

'I'm sorry, ladies and gentlemen, that was the owner. An offer has been accepted and this apartment is now off the market. If you'd like a list of the other places I'm able to show you in this area, please ask me on your way out.'

With a flurry of tutting and head-shaking, the well-heeled New Yorkers deserted the apartment. Seeing the place emptied, Luke decided that it wasn't just cool, it was cold. He wasn't sure how much time he would spend here.

The realtor focused her tight smile on Luke's mother.

'Ms Jennings, I presume?'

'Call me Crystal.'

'Congratulations, Crystal. All this is yours.'

Luke wondered who his mother had called on the phone.

Nine

SCOTLAND

'Did you get the note I slid under your door?' Mrs Duncan asked, as she drove Megan to the hospital. 'I was worried about you.'

'Yes. I'm sorry. I must have been so tired that your knocking didn't wake me.'

'Obviously a good night's sleep was what you needed most. You say you haven't been well?'

'No. I've been in hospital, but they couldn't say what was wrong with me.'

'The kind of stress you've been under often has a physical effect.'

'I guess . . .' Megan didn't want to mention the poison theory. The Head already thought Megan was being paranoid because she was sure somebody had tried to run her over.

'It's good of you to come in with me,' Megan said instead.

'I like to visit Grace. But don't worry, I will leave the two of you alone. I'll arrange for you to be collected safely and brought back to the school.'

'Thanks. What happened to my helicopter?'

'The pilot told Security that he was needed elsewhere.'

'I see.' Could Megan summon the helicopter back to take her home later? It seemed extravagant. And what if she were refused? She would leave it until later in the day, when it became business hours, New York time, then call Uncle Mike.

At the hospital, Grace was delighted to see her. Both of her legs were elevated. Megan could only hug her friend awkwardly.

'What's the latest?'

'Broken in five places. It'll be a long time before I ride a bike again. But at least I'm alive, thanks to you.'

'Don't say that.' Conscious of Mrs Duncan standing behind her, Megan changed the subject. 'Why aren't you in London, with your mum and dad?'

'They're going to move me soon, when Parliament's in recess. In the meantime, I'm safer here. Mum's worried. In the past, MPs' children have never been fair game for terrorists. Today, it seems like anything goes. But that's enough about me. I was so sorry to hear about your dad . . .'

Megan told Grace what little she knew about Jack Kite's death. Frustratingly, the Head was there all the time, listening to their conversation.

'Now this eco-terrorist group is claiming responsibility, but nobody's heard of them before.'

'Why would they do that?'

'Something to do with chemical weapons.'

After twenty minutes, Mrs Duncan excused herself, saying that she had some errands.

'I'll take a taxi back to the school. You can use the car, Megan.'

'Thanks, I appreciate it.'

'Blimey,' said Grace when the Head was out of earshot. 'I thought she'd never go. And leaving you her car – why the red carpet treatment?'

Now Megan told her everything that had happened, including the attempted poisoning and how she was sure that she had been the hit-and-run driver's target, not Grace.

'It makes sense,' Grace said. 'I mean, my mum's important, but she's only the Pensions Minister. You don't get old people threatening to kill an MP's kids because she didn't raise their pension above the rate of inflation.'

'But I'm not sure I buy this "software for chemical weapons" story either,' Megan said.

'Why else would someone have it in for you?'

'I don't know.'

'If there's anything I can do to help . . . I don't feel a lot of use, here in bed.'

'Just talking to you helps. I'm sorry I didn't call earlier.'

'Don't worry. It's complicated, phoning in hospitals. And you came in person. That's a hundred times better. What's it like, being in our old room with everyone else gone?'

'Really, really weird. All your stuff's there but you never will be again, that's the weirdest thing.'

'Anything of mine you want to use, feel free.'

'Thanks.'

'I'm not going anywhere for a while.'

'Maybe I'll stick around too,' Megan said. 'I'm as

safe here as I am anywhere else. I've got a lot of things to think about.'

'Like what?'

Megan told her about how she would inherit most of Dad's estate in a few weeks' time.

'That's mega! You're going to be one of the richest people in the world!'

'I feel bad about Luke, though. Why should I get it all?'

'Being rich stops some people from doing anything useful, my mum says. Maybe your dad thought all that money would have a bad effect on Luke.'

'It's possible.' More than possible, Megan admitted to herself, presuming that Dad thought about Luke when he was making his will in the first place. Generally, Jack Kite only talked about his son when Megan brought the subject up.

'What have the police said to you?' Megan asked. 'Do they have a theory about who tried to run us over?'

'Zilch. They kept looking at me as though I was only telling half the story. But half the story is all I know.'

Lunchtime came and the hospital began to clear out visitors.

'Where will you go?' Grace asked Megan.

'I have no idea.'

In the car, Megan tried to relax. This landscape, with its rolling, purple heathered hills and wide, open sky, had always made her feel centred. Today she was preoccupied and only started to take in the scenery when they approached the blind hill where she and Grace had nearly been killed. The mirror on the tree at the top of the hill showed that nothing was coming the other way. Nevertheless, Megan gripped the side of her seat. The driver asked if she was all right. She nodded. The moment passed.

Where should she go? Back at school, Megan packed a bag with light, summer clothes. Then she rang Tom Morris.

'Tom, this is Megan Kite. I'm at Brunts. I want to know if it's safe for me to leave the school, whether there's a threat from these so-called environmental terrorists.'

'The police say that there's no evidence these terrorists are real, Miss Kite. I think they're jokers, looking to publicize their cause on the back of your father's dreadful accident.'

'So it's safe for me to return?'

'I can provide you with full-time security if you desire it. I need to talk with your uncle before putting your new security regime into place. He was too busy to see me yesterday.'

'OK, let's discuss that when I'm back in London.'

Did she want a full-time bodyguard? It would feel awkward, but maybe it was necessary. There was, however, one thing she definitely did want.

'Tom, have somebody sweep the London apartment, would you? And have it done carefully. I was taken ill there, that's why I missed Dad's memorial service.'

She told him what the doctor had said and gave him the hospital contact information.

'If it was this BZ stuff, Dad's flat is the only place I could have been exposed.'

'OK, I'll talk to the hospital and the police. Then I'll sweep the place myself, ASAP, before you get here. Do you want me to send a helicopter?'

'No, it'll be quicker to take a scheduled flight from Edinburgh. I'll let you know when I'm landing – maybe you could meet me at the airport?'

'Of course, Miss Kite. And I'll make sure that the flat is fully secured for your arrival.'

'Thanks, Tom.'

Megan had known the security chief for as long as she could remember. She would be returning to someone she could trust.

Megan rang the school office and asked if they would arrange her flight to London. Then she keyed in the combination of the safe where she kept her spare plastic cards and passport. Before the door could spring open, her mobile rang. It was the Head.

'Megan, there's a flight to London you can make if you leave straight away. Otherwise there'll be a two-hour wait. Do you want my car to take you?'

'Please!'

Megan grabbed the wallet and her emergency cash stash and shoved them into her purse. She relocked the safe and threw her bag over her shoulder. The rest of her stuff was in a carry-on case. From Dad she had learned that it didn't matter what class you travelled in, airport baggage systems were prone to theft and sloppiness. If you travelled light enough, you could save loads of time when you got off the plane by not having to wait for your bags to be unloaded.

In the car to the airport, Megan phoned her Uncle Mike. It was half past eight in New York and he had just arrived at the office. Francis put her straight through to him. Her uncle's voice was warm, comforting.

'Megan, how are you holding up?'

'Not too bad, thanks. I've been sleeping a lot, for some reason.'

'That's natural with grief, Megan. I'm sorry I had to hurry back to the States so quickly. Kite Industries is in a bit of a meltdown at the moment. It's taking all my time to keep things under control.'

'I ought to thank you for looking after my inheritance.'

'No need. In the long term, Kite's software is recession proof. We make good stuff. Everyone needs us. That's why we'll remain one of the world's most profitable companies, no matter how volatile the world markets are. But Jack's death makes us look weak. Share prices will tumble for a while, but they'll go back up when investors realize that it's business as usual. By the way, did somebody tell you about the will's contents?'

'Crystal gave me a brief outline.'

'Probably a slanted one. Crystal thought that Luke ought to get Kite Industries shares but Jack was very specific about what he wanted. Luke has to make his own way in the world. There's a trust fund that will see him through college and give him a good pay out when he graduates. He's a very lucky guy.'

'But why do I deserve to get all the rest?'

'Because . . . this isn't the time or place, Megan, but you were a wanted child, a planned child. Also, your father hoped that you would choose to be involved in the business.'

'If I do get involved, it won't be until I've had my gap year and done my degree. Four years.'

'Fine. Now, about this chemical weapons nonsense. I've

looked into this ACW group. They don't—'

'Hold on.' Megan told him what she had told Tom Morris about the suspected poisoning. Mike sounded very disturbed.

'I'll talk to Tom as soon as I get off the phone with you. And I'll have our investigators look into how you could have come into contact with – what did you say the stuff was called?'

'I can't remember the full name. BZ for short. Mike, are we involved with software for detonating chemical weapons?'

'Not directly, but it's possible secondary sellers are reselling some of our products for purposes that they weren't intended for. I'm looking into that, too, Megan. It's not the kind of publicity we need. Especially not at the moment.'

'No! I'm relieved you feel that way.'

'What will you do now?'

'Go back to the flat. Then I think I'd better talk to the police, get their side of things. After which, I might come and visit you in Manhattan. I could use a break. And I could use a good talk about the future.'

'Please come. I'd love to spend time with you. And if there is a real threat, I can protect you better here than in the UK. I'm so sorry I'm not with you now.'

'Don't worry,' Megan reassured her uncle. 'Business always has come first in our family.'

Ten

'Can we move in today?' Luke asked Crystal over breakfast. He ate two chocolate muffins while Mom chewed organic muesli.

'It'll be a week or two. I have to sign papers and get the owner to redecorate before we move in.'

'But the place is fine as it is.'

'Sweetie, it's so *male*. And wooden floors are fine in the living spaces but I want a pile carpet in my bedroom, don't you?'

'I don't want to live in a hotel room, is all. I might see if I can stay with a friend for a few days.'

'Fine by me, but the insurance company is paying for our rooms, so don't think I'll stump up what you save on the room for spending money.'

'I've got money,' Luke said.

'What are you going to do today?'

'I thought I'd head home, look up a couple of people, maybe see what kind of mess the gas leak made of our building.'

'You don't mind if I don't come with you?' Mom asked.

'Not at all,' said Luke, who would much rather that she didn't.

Luke's bike was still where he'd left it, locked to some railings just down from the hotel. Luke rode over to Sixth Street and hauled his bike down the stairs. You weren't allowed to lift a bike over the high entrance turnstiles, so he had to haul it back up, then ride to a bigger station on Broadway. That was OK. It was a nice morning and this line had better connections. Luke only had to change station once, but it was a pain carrying the bike up another set of steep stairs. He wouldn't like to do that in rush hour.

Kal Delgado lived near the subway on Seventh Avenue, so Luke visited him first. Nobody home. There was mail piled up inside the front door. Looked like the whole family was out of town. Time, then, to head to the apartment. It was uphill all the way, through wide. uncrowded streets, less rich but less busy than Manhattan. Home.

In the movies, when people visited their burned-out homes, there was always some sentimental item left out in the debris: a picture, a childhood doll, maybe some kind of sports souvenir. Luke hoped to find something significant, but couldn't think what. He cycled past Dave's bicycle shop and considered buying himself a better lock, now that he was living in high-crime Manhattan. Then he turned the corner and saw what had happened to their building.

It was gutted. The ground floor, where the Kellermans lived, was more or less intact, but boarded up. The first floor, which Luke shared with Crystal, was gone. There were some metal girders, rusty brown and twisted, poking into the air, but where he had lived, nothing remained. What had happened to Pete and Irwin, the couple who shared the third floor? They would have been at work when it happened.

They must have lost everything too.

'My, my, Luke Kite on a bike. What are you doing here, dude?'

It was Andy Smith, from school. Andy and Luke were neighbours and had been close friends when they were kids, then drifted apart after fifth grade.

'I'm inspecting the ruins of my territory. For the first time.'

'But that happened, like, a week ago.'

'I've been out of the country. My dad . . .'

Andy had obviously missed the news about Jack Kite and Luke didn't feel like filling him in.

'Oh, right, visiting your dad. Well, you picked a good time not to be home.'

'The police said it was some kind of gas leak?'

'Funny kind of gas leak if you ask me. I heard the place go up. There were, like, three explosions really close to each other. Does that sound like a gas leak?'

'I wouldn't know.'

'Where are you staying?'

'This old hotel in Greenwich Village.'

'Long way from home.'

'Tell me about it. There's not much action back here either. Nobody seems to be around. How come you're here?'

'Work. My mom and sister are staying on Long Island for the summer. I'm meant to be going there at weekends but I've got an internship at a video company so they're letting me stick around the apartment on my own. My dad looks in most days but you know how flakey he is. Pretty much got the place to myself. So if you ever need a place to crash . . .'

'Cool. You working today?'

'Meant to be, but there's not a lot to do. They're waiting on a contract. Feel like playing some games?'

'Now you're talking,' Luke said.

He followed his friend around the corner without a backward glance.

LONDON

Megan took a taxi from the airport to the Barbican. She could have got a Kite Industries car to meet her. But why wait? She was about to become ridiculously, humongously rich. She could do what she wanted. And it was nice to be anonymous.

Dad made a show of not being bothered about money and he had passed this attitude on to Megan. Once you had enough to live comfortably, Dad said, too much money was more of a responsibility than it was a reward. Don't let the government tax too much of it, but don't be mean either, that was Dad's philosophy. He gave to charity quietly and paid other people to deal with any hassles that he didn't want to deal with himself.

Dad was dead. She didn't want to spend time in the Barbican flat. It would keep reminding her of what had happened. She needed to keep busy, to find a way to work through the grief. Going to Africa would probably be the best thing, but, first, she needed to see Uncle Mike, to sort things out. And she ought to spend more time with Luke. Those two were the only family she had now.

Whatever Tom told her, Megan decided, she would pick up some stuff and fly to New York straight away. What was the point of hanging around in London, being miserable? With Grace stuck in Scotland, she'd rather be on the move. Let Tom deal with the police. There was nothing she could tell them. There were more hospital tests but they had hospitals in the US. If she felt ill again, she could get a check-up. Megan rang Mike on his mobile. The call went straight to voicemail.

'It's Megan. I'm back in London. I'm about to stop at Dad's flat to collect some stuff, then I'm going to come to New York to see you and Luke, like you suggested. Is it OK if I stay with you? Talk soon. Bye.'

The taxi reached the Barbican.

'Wait for me here,' Megan told the driver, leaving her bags. 'I'm going straight back to the airport.'

She let herself into the building and took the lift up to the penthouse. After several floors, the lift stopped. Megan got off as another person got on. She didn't recognize the person who nodded at her. Afterwards she would remember a girl roughly her own age, definitely wearing blue jeans, possibly a white top. But Megan wasn't concentrating, so it could have been a fake memory. There was only one other penthouse on this floor and its occupants were a couple in their seventies. Megan assumed the girl was visiting them.

Except, Megan realized, this wasn't the right floor. She had got out a floor too early. She had pressed the right button, so the girl who got in would have gone up before going down. The only way to the top floor was by the lift, so Megan pressed the call button again. I'm so distracted,

Megan thought. I don't even know what day of the week it is, never mind what floor I'm on.

The lift only took a few seconds to come back. It was bound to be going down to the ground floor first. Megan decided to get in anyway. Better than standing here like a lemon. The door opened. Megan stepped inside, surprised to find it empty. Then she saw the young woman who'd just got into the lift. She was lying on the floor. Her top was drenched in blood. She'd been shot in the head. On the penthouse floor. Megan's mouth opened and closed, but no sound came out. The dead girl should have been her.

The lift continued its downward journey. The door opened on the ground floor. How long would it take before the killer or killers realized their mistake? Why had they killed the girl in the lift rather than waiting for Megan to enter the apartment? Megan had to get out of the building. The killer was still up there. But Megan couldn't abandon the girl in the lift.

Before stepping out of the lift, Megan pressed the emergency button. Then, head down, she hurried to the exit and let herself out.

'No bags, miss?'

'Pardon?'

'I thought you were going back to the flat to collect a bag?'

'Changed my mind.'

'Where to?'

'Heathrow.'

BROOKLYN

Luke hadn't been in Andy's house since fifth grade, but the place had hardly changed. It was a tumbledown brownstone which was too big for three people. They stayed because Andy's mom had been awarded it in her divorce settlement and the schools nearby were good.

'Maybe you could lodge here,' Andy said, after Luke had told him about Dad's death, the explosion, Crystal's new place. 'Stick at the same school. You don't wanna go to some snooty private school in Manhattan.'

'You could be right,' Luke said. He was fuzzy on the details of his trust fund but figured the less was spent on his education, the more there would be for him to enjoy when he was twenty-one.

'So, what do you wanna play?'

'What you got?'

They whiled away the day playing a bank robbery simulation game, then shooting pool in the basement. The pool table was another new addition and Luke found himself tempted to move in here. But Crystal would be offended. She was clingy. Except when she had a boyfriend. Then she treated Luke like something that was stuck to her shoe and she couldn't brush off. That was why she wanted to live in the Village, Luke figured. She was after a rich boyfriend while she could still pass for thirty. The less Luke was around, the easier she would find that.

'What kind of rent would your mom charge?' he asked Andy.

LONDON

Megan's first thought was to phone Mike. She tried his Kite Industries direct line.

'Your uncle's not in the office,' Francis told her. 'He's due back in a couple of hours. Can I help you?'

'Ask him to call me,' Megan said, and hung up.

She couldn't decide whether to call Tom Morris. She was terrified of what she would find. Her best bet, Megan decided, was to go to the police. She was about to tell the driver to forget Heathrow, to head for Scotland Yard. Then her mobile rang. The display showed that the caller was Tom Morris. She accepted the call but didn't speak.

'Hello?' The speaker sounded American. 'Who is this?'

The speaker wasn't Tom. It was someone very different. Megan could hear it in his voice. This was the man who had killed the girl in the lift. He was using Tom's phone, which meant that he had probably killed Tom, too. Megan put on a Home Counties accent.

'This is Constable Shawcross of the Metropolitan Police. To whom am I speaking?'

The connection was instantly cut. Let the killer think that he had killed the right girl. Let him think that Megan was dead. Her cab was more than halfway to Heathrow. She could talk to the police there. Or in New York. London no longer felt safe. Megan needed to be with her uncle and her brother.

The journey passed in frozen seconds. Megan was unable to calculate what she needed to do. All she knew was that she needed to escape. Somebody had tried to kill her, twice. And they had succeeded in murdering her dad.

'Which terminal, miss?'

'Five.' Megan gave the driver a generous tip, but not so generous that he was bound to remember her. Then she hurried to the BA Reservations desk.

'I'd like to book a seat on the next flight to New York,' she said.

'Certainly. JFK or Newark?'

'Whichever's going first.'

'There's a flight to JFK in fifty minutes. If you only have carry-on luggage, you'll make it. Is that all you have with you?'

'This is all,' Megan said. From the carry-on bag, she pulled out her blue wallet, which she hadn't touched since leaving Scotland that morning. It felt lighter than usual.

'First Class, Club Class, or Economy?'

'Club,' Megan said. She would feel too conspicuous in First, but couldn't handle going Economy.

'How would you like to pay?'

'Visa.' When Megan reached for her platinum card she understood why the wallet felt so light. Her credit cards weren't there. Neither was her passport. She had the wrong wallet.

Eleven

The game took longer than usual. Andy was a good opponent and aced the final stage.

'I'll get you next time,' Luke said. 'Now I suppose I should be getting back.'

'The connections to the Village are really slow this time of night. You'd be better off staying here.'

'What time is it?'

'Nearly midnight.'

Luke swore. Crystal would be asleep but he turned on his phone and texted her anyway. STAIN@FRENZ, BK TMRW XL. No point in mentioning Andy, she wouldn't remember who he was.

'Wanna watch some crap on TV?'

'Why not?'

Luke went to the bathroom. When he came back the widescreen plasma was showing CNN.

'What other channels you got?' he asked.

'Hold your horses, dude, you might want to watch this.'

'*In breaking news, tragedy stalks the family of one of the world's richest men. Following the unexplained death of her father in a helicopter crash, seventeen-year-old Megan Kite has been murdered in what police describe as a robbery gone wrong. The body of Megan Kite was found in an elevator outside the London Barbican home that she inherited from her father. Thieves had forced their way into the penthouse apartment, intent on robbery. Reports suggest that, as the assailants prepared to make their escape, they ran into Ms Kite in the elevator and panicked. Billionaire Jack Kite also had one son, sixteen-year-old Luke, who lives in Brooklyn.*

'This is really heavy,' Andy said. 'I'm sorry, man.'

Luke shook his head. Megan. Dead. He couldn't take it in. He stared numbly at the screen.

'Your phone was vibrating while you were out of the room,' Andy told him.

Luke killed the TV sound and listened to his messages, all of which had come during the two hours in which he'd had his phone switched off so as not to interrupt their game. Three from Crystal, wondering where he was. The third clearly came after the news.

'Luke, I have something terrible to tell you. Please call, whatever the time.'

'What are you going to do?' Andy asked. 'Go home?'

'After what just happened to Megan, and what they did to our apartment? I don't know who these guys are who got Megan, but they're probably after me, too.'

'And what's all this stuff about your dad?'

Luke told him. 'Andy, can I stay here? I mean, without telling anyone, anyone at all?'

'Sure you can. I won't even tell my mom. But are you OK? I mean, you just lost your dad and sister.'

Luke wished he could cry, but he felt too numb. His emotions were shutting down. He had to be strong. He had to fight and to do that he had to be numb. If he allowed himself to be sad, he would also have to allow himself to be terrified.

Economy Class wasn't as bad as Megan feared. It was probably worse if you were her dad, who was six foot one, but she was only five foot seven, so had enough leg room. And the flight wasn't full, so she had space to stretch out.

'Excuse me, Miss Thompson? Miss Thompson?'

Megan remembered that she was travelling on her friend's passport.

'You requested a vegetarian meal?'

'Oh, thanks.'

The food looked uninspiring, compared to what she usually got in First Class. Megan didn't know her friend's credit limit, so had taken the cheaper option. She would explain to Grace as soon as she could. Megan knew Grace's PIN number, so using the card to pay for the ticket had been no problem.

Nobody had questioned Megan's masquerade as Grace. The two looked similar enough for a poor passport photo to fool officials.

There were definite advantages to being Grace Thompson, at least until her credit card bills started to arrive. Those went straight to the home of her parents, the Pensions Minister and the MEP.

When Megan arrived in New York it was only dusk, but it was 2 a.m. by her body clock. Immigration took her fingerprint, but that was to make sure that she was the same person when she left the country, not to check who she was in the first place.

Megan got out her mobile to call her uncle. Then she realized that, as soon as she turned it on, anybody with access to the mobile network would be able to find out where she was. Paranoid? Not when two people – probably three, if they got Tom too – were already dead. Instead of getting a cab into Manhattan, she asked the driver if he knew of a cheap place in Queen's that took credit cards.

'And if you don't have any cash, how were you planning to pay me?'

'London cabs take credit cards.'

'This is not London,' said the Indian driver.

Megan had her friend's credit card but she didn't have a cash card. She was going to have to find a way to raise some money. She looked in her purse.

'I've got some euros or some sterling. I'll tip well.'

She ended up giving him a twenty-euro note and getting five dollars' change, which would allow her to buy a subway ticket in the morning. Welcome to poverty, she told herself, as she settled into a narrow, single room with noisy air-conditioning, no mini-bar and a TV that only had the ad-ridden free-to-view channels.

At least the hotel had free coffee and muffins. After having a shower in the morning, Megan flicked through a copy of *USA Today* over breakfast. Nothing about Dad. He was old news now. She checked out and queued for a single subway ticket.

'Buy a ten-ride pass and you get two rides free,' the

woman in the booth explained.

'No, thanks,' Megan said. She didn't explain that she barely had enough cash to cover even a single ticket. This would be her first ride on a New York subway. And, hopefully, her last.

The E-train came quickly. The grey, metallic trains were as dull and functional as London's tubes, and just as crowded. Being rush hour, it was impossible to find a seat. Megan was jostled and pressed up against and given tetchy glances for daring to have a bag at her feet where other people could be standing. After the long haul into Manhattan, she had to change at the Port Authority in order to get a train that stopped near Kite Industries' headquarters. It was gone nine by now and there were fewer commuters and not too many tourists. She sat down and thought through what would happen next.

The train pulled into the station. Megan slung her canvas bag over her left shoulder and hurried on to the platform. But for the anxiety in her eyes she could be any anonymous Brit on a shopping trip. Unless someone here was after her. In which case, the next few minutes would be the most dangerous of all. She had her hair tied back and wore sunglasses but should have disguised herself better. For this was the one place in the world that she could be expected to come. Until she got inside the Kite Building, she was vulnerable.

Luke took the subway to Manhattan. His first thought was to go to the hotel but it was only nine. Crystal wouldn't be awake yet. Neither would he, normally, but he had slept badly, mourning his sister. He was trying to be tough about it. After all, he didn't know Megan well. Over the course of his sixteen years, they had spent – at most – a month together. They had both lost a father, and now he had lost her too. Whatever chance they had to be friends, to become a true brother and sister, was gone for good.

He bought a paper. The news about Megan had broken too late for the early editions, but the *New York Post* had it. There was little in their story that Luke didn't already know. The *Post* noted that Megan was to inherit a majority shareholding in Kite Industries on her eighteenth birthday and the uncertainty created by her death would cause the company's stock to fall further. That didn't bother Luke. He had no Kite stock. But he'd like to know who got Megan's shares now she was dead.

Luke turned on to Madison Avenue and his heart stopped. There, at the edge of the wide, busy road, right outside the Kite building, stood a ghost.

Twelve

The security guard inspected her bag.

'Thinking of moving in here, were you, ma'am?'

Megan smiled. 'In a manner of speaking, yes.'

'You're good to go.'

In Reception there were a bank of TVs to entertain the people queuing for attention. There was no sound: that would be too distracting. Megan glanced at the screens. A supermodel had been caught shoplifting. There were forest fires somewhere in the midwest. In business news . . .

'Can I help you, Miss?' said a smart blonde sat behind the long, semi-circular desk.

'My name's Megan Kite. I'm here to see my uncle, Mike.'

Megan was expecting the usual sycophantic behaviour that greeted the boss's daughter. Instead, the woman behind the desk gave her an incredulous, disgusted look.

'*What* did you say?'

'I said my name's Megan Kite. I—'

'How do you have the nerve, on a day like today, to come in and be so . . . I can't find the word for it. Is this some kind of sick, British humour?'

'I don't . . .'

'We are *in mourning* here. Now, you get out of this office before I call Security.'

Megan stared. Then the receptionist glanced at the screens to her right. They were showing a picture of Megan, aged thirteen, a picture that she had forgotten existed. No wonder the woman didn't recognize her. Those freckles had long since faded. That was the year that she had dyed her hair blonde. But the photo wasn't what arrested Megan's attention. It was the words scrolling beneath it. *Heiress murdered at father's London apartment. Tragedy stalks Kite family.*

'Are you still here? Security!'

'I'm going, I'm going!'

Megan charged past the security guard, out of the building. On Madison Avenue, she stood for a minute, trying to stop herself from shaking. Why did the world think she was dead? The girl in the lift looked nothing like her. There was no way anyone would have confused one for the other. Unless they wanted to. They were about the same age, the same height and the same colour. The girl had fair hair though. Or was it light brown?

'Megan?'

She turned to see her brother, wearing old combat trousers, sneakers and a *Public Enemy* T-shirt. He looked dazed.

'Is it really you?'

She nodded, slowly. 'They think I'm dead. But it was someone else. I saw her body.'

'Are you here to see Mike?'

'They won't let me in,' Megan explained.

'You can't stay outside. I don't think either of us is safe.'

'No, I suppose not. I don't have any money, Luke. I only have what's in this bag. I don't live anywhere and people are trying to kill me. What the hell am I going to do?'

'I could take you in, vouch for you.'

'Do they know you in there?'

Luke shook his head. 'I never came to see Uncle Mike at work.'

Megan held back from crying, but she could feel her panic rising. 'Let's start by getting away. I don't know who's after us, but this is the first place they're going to look.'

Luke hailed a yellow cab. 'Washington Square Hotel.'

'Why are we going there?' Megan asked.

'I'll explain when you've told me why you aren't dead.'

Megan summed up what had happened in London.

'But how can they have mistaken this girl for you?'

'I don't know. Maybe somebody deliberately misidentified the body, somebody who wanted me out of the way.'

'Then who knows you're still alive?'

'Whoever killed Tom and that girl. And you.'

'Maybe you'll be safer if we let the rest of the world keep thinking you're dead.'

'How come? How long for?'

'I'm not sure. Listen, there's something I haven't told you. It's why we're staying in a hotel.'

'Why?'

'Somebody blew up our apartment.'

Luke told her what had happened. Megan struggled to take it in. 'Dad, me, you. Somebody wants to kill all of us. We need protection. We need to talk to Uncle Mike.

And I couldn't even get into the building.'

'Why didn't you show them some proof of identity? I mean, you're you. Uncle Mike knows you!'

'It's mad I know, but I don't have any ID on me.' Megan didn't try to explain why this was. It made her sound so flaky. 'Who does Uncle Mike think was behind the explosion?'

'The official story is that it was a gas leak. But, after what happened to you . . .'

'It must be true, then,' Megan told her brother. 'We are terrorist targets.'

'If we are, Uncle Mike is, too.'

'I'll call him when we get to the hotel.'

Usually, Greenwich Village was Megan's favourite New York haunt. It was full of quirky stores and, despite all the tourists, still felt like a neighbourhood. The houses might be owned by millionaires these days, but you could still feel the area's bohemian past. Dad sometimes talked about buying an apartment here, but never did. He wasn't one of those people with a house on every continent. Two homes was enough for him. When he was in New York, Dad used one of Kite Industries' hospitality apartments.

'If people are after us, isn't this rather a conspicuous area?' Megan asked, as they pulled up outside the Washington Square Hotel with its old fashioned railings and Art Deco signage, a stone's throw from Washington Square Park.

'I didn't choose it, Mom did.'

'What's our first move?' Megan asked.

'I need to collect my stuff and talk to my mom,' Luke said, paying the fare. 'Then we call Mike, yeah?'

'OK. I'll wait in the café.'

Megan got a table to herself and ordered a double latté. She realized that she was really hungry, so ordered cheesecake. Comfort food. She ought to go for something healthier but needed a sugar rush. Also, she remembered, she needed money. If Luke didn't return, she wouldn't be able to pay the tab.

But Luke would return. Why wouldn't he? He was family. Her latté arrived. The caffeine sent Megan's mind into overdrive. Luke's mother was upstairs and she wasn't family. If Megan were killed, would Luke inherit her shares in Kite Industries? That would be motive enough for murder. Megan tried to piece together what Luke had told her about the explosion. Crystal wasn't home, hadn't been all afternoon. It happened five minutes after Luke had left the building. So Luke could have been a target, but his mother wasn't.

Megan tried to work out the timings. He'd got her text, Luke had said, just before the bomb went off. Megan had sent that text a few minutes before she went on the cycle ride, where someone tried to run her over. So someone or some group tried to kill both of them at exactly the same time. Then they tried to kill her again. This wasn't the caffeine rush speaking: they were both in terrible danger.

Crystal wasn't home. Luke thought about phoning her but decided to get his stuff together first – what little of it there was. His phone rang. Andy.

'So what's the score? I'm about to head into work. Are you planning on moving in here?'

Instant decision time. Maybe Mike would sort them out somewhere safe, but, until then, going to Andy's was safer than staying with Crystal.

'If it's still OK with you. I'm just collecting my stuff.'

Best not to tell Andy about Megan. Yet.

'You didn't take a key, didja?'

'No.'

'I'm off to work but I'll leave a front-door key under the trash can. They don't collect until tomorrow. But you'll need the burglar alarm code. I promised my mom I'd always put it on when there was nobody home. Otherwise we're not insured.'

'Fine.' Luke wrote the code down. 'What time do you get home?'

'Four, five, six, depends how busy we are.'

'OK if I bring a friend over?'

'If she's got a friend for me.'

Luke laughed. 'I'll ask her. Later, dude.'

He took the elevator down and left his key at the desk. 'I'm checking out but there's still some stuff in the room. My mom'll sort it out.'

'Thank you, sir.'

He joined Megan in the coffee shop. She looked anxious.

'What's wrong?'

'Nothing's wrong, except I've finished my coffee and cake and don't have enough money to pay.'

'I'm here now. Want another coffee?'

'No thanks, I'm wired enough already. A juice maybe.'

Luke ordered them both an orange juice. Megan looked tired, vulnerable. He enjoyed playing the big brother for once.

79

'I think I've got a place for us to stay until Uncle Mike sorts out the situation.'

Megan looked uncomfortable. 'Where?'

'A friend in Brooklyn.'

'I think I'd rather stay with Uncle Mike.'

'OK,' Luke said. 'Call him. Got your phone with you?'

'I have, but I'm paranoid. The killers know my number. If I use it, whoever tried to kill me might be able to track me here.'

'Use mine. Then only Uncle Mike will know.'

'I guess.' She reached for the phone. 'Maybe you should speak to him first. He'll freak out when he hears my voice.'

Before Luke could reply, the phone began to ring.

Thirteen

'It's Crystal,' he said, looking at the display.

'Don't tell her about me,' Megan warned. She didn't want his mother knowing her business. Fair enough,

'OK.' He pressed 'receive'. 'Hi, Mom.'

'Where are you?'

'I'm at West Fourteenth,' Luke fibbed, 'heading down the subway to get back to Brooklyn. Where are you?'

'I'm at the hotel. They tell me you've taken all your stuff.'

'Nearly all of it, yeah. I thought I'd stay with Kal until the apartment's ready. But I can come back if you want.'

'It's OK. No need. Do you have Kal's home number?'

'Not on me, but what's it matter? You've got my cell.'

'I ought to call and check that it's OK with his parents,' Crystal said, which was rich, considering how she usually avoided contact with any of his friends' parents. Thing was, they might want her to return their hospitality.

'It's fine, there's no need to call. Listen, I wondered if you'd seen Uncle Mike. There's been some news.'

'You heard about Megan already. I'm so sorry, hon.'

Luke took a deep breath. He was usually good at fooling his mom but couldn't decide how upset he was supposed to sound. 'Yes, it's really sad. But Megan would want us to carry

81

on, I'm sure.' He stood. 'First I need to talk to Mike so I can find out the funeral details.'

'I think the funeral will be in London.'

'Oh. Right.'

'At a time like this, I wish you were with me, Luke.'

'I would be, but I'm feeling paranoid, Mom. Somebody tried to kill me. They succeeded in killing my sister. Don't you think I should be in hiding?'

'I suppose Brooklyn's safer than a hotel, at least until the apartment's ready. Hasn't your uncle been in touch at all?'

'Not since I got back. According to . . .' Luke was about to say 'according to Megan' but stopped himself in time. '. . . the *New York Times*, Kite Industries is in serious trouble. Maybe I should call him.'

'Maybe you should, but I'd wait until office hours are over. I've got to go, sweetie. I'm having my eyebrows threaded.'

'OK. Talk later.'

He hung up and began to tell Megan about the conversation.

'Ssssh.'

'What?'

'Look behind you.'

Luke did as he was told. There was his mother, getting into a sleek, black limousine with shaded windows. A capped and suited driver closed the door for her before setting off.

'Where did she say she was going?' Megan asked.

Luke told her. Megan grimaced.

'I know she's your mother and all, but I don't trust her as far as I can throw her.'

Luke couldn't argue with Megan. Crystal was always in it for herself. His whole life, Luke's needs had come a distant second. Third, if she had a guy on the go.

'There's something going on,' he said. 'Crystal told me to leave it a while before calling Mike, but I'm going to do it now.'

'Good idea,' Megan said. 'Then I can talk to him, too.'

'That'll certainly grab his attention, speaking to a dead girl.'

Megan smiled. 'Maybe you'd better break it to him gently.'

His uncle's phone went straight to voicemail.

'This is Luke,' he said. 'We need to talk.'

Megan hardly knew Brooklyn. According to Luke, if this borough was a city, it would be the fourth largest in the US. It was far bigger than the island of Manhattan. The borough's borders hugged the right-hand side of The Narrows, the tidal strait beneath which the subway ran.

The subway journey was crowded, speeding them out of one city and into another. Once they were across the river, Luke and Megan had to change to the Brighton Line. This time the carriage was less full and Megan had the space to think.

Was Uncle Mike in hiding? Was that why he hadn't been in touch? They got out at the Prospect Park subway at Flatbush Avenue and Empire Boulevard.

'Been here before?' Luke asked, making conversation to relax her. He pointed at the vast park. Megan shook her head. 'The park was designed by the same guys who did Central Park, directly afterwards.'

'Right.' Megan wasn't in the mood to look round a park.

'Most people who visit think it's better. But most people

didn't come here, which is why Brooklyn should be a good place to hide.'

'I hope so,' Megan mumbled.

They headed downtown. Luke pointed out Dixon's bicycle shop. On the yellow outside wall was a large painting of an elegant black couple riding a tandem, she holding a parasol, him trailing three balloons. The woman was in the front seat. Megan liked that.

'Did you lose your bike in the explosion?' she asked Luke.

'No, I was riding it at the time. I brought it over here yesterday.'

'So, who's this "Kal" we're staying with?'

'Kal's in Europe. We're staying with another friend.'

Megan was confused. 'Do you always lie to your mother?'

'Wouldn't you? I've learned not to trust anyone, even family.'

'Even me?'

Luke didn't reply. He turned on to a tree-lined road. 'Wait here.'

Megan pretended to examine a notice about a lost cat called 'Hilly'. Luke leaned down and retrieved a key from somewhere out of sight. When he'd let himself in, Megan hurried to join him. The less time she spent lingering on the street, the better. She heard him punch a key code into the alarm system of the dingy, dark house. This was where they were going to hide, in a house that smelled of stale socks.

Luke's phone began to ring.

'Luke. Sorry I didn't call you earlier.' It was good to hear his uncle's transatlantic tones. 'It's hard to keep up at the moment.'

On hearing his uncle's voice, Luke began to lose it. 'I'm really scared, Mike. Someone tried to kill me. Now I hear someone's killed Megan.'

'Don't take that as read, Luke. I've been talking to our people in London. They're saying that the press jumped the gun with the news of Megan's death. Nobody who knows her has made a positive ID of Megan.'

Now was the time to tell Mike that his niece was alive, but, for some reason, Luke held back.

'I don't understand. Surely the police could tell if it was her?'

For a moment, his uncle's usual calm seemed to break. Luke's sister stood close to him but not so close that she could hear every word. Which was probably a good thing.

'She was shot in the head, evidently. So they can't be sure. You said someone tried to kill you. Your mother told me about the gas explosion. Is that what you mean?'

'I don't think it was a gas explosion. I think it was a bomb. Somebody wanted me dead.'

'Don't be so melodramatic, Luke. Why would anyone want to kill you?'

'Because they blame me by association for this military software thing? Do you buy that story?'

'Tom Morris was looking into it. When we last spoke, he said there was no evidence that the environmental group, the ACW, even existed. Those kind of groups don't tend to use terrorist methods. It alienates their supporters. Most likely what happened in London was a robbery gone wrong. The burglars read about Jack's death, thought the place would be empty and panicked when Megan interrupted them.'

That didn't fit with what Megan said had happened, but before Luke could turn the conversation round, Mike changed the subject.

'Your mother rang me. She wanted to find out if, with Megan gone, you stood to inherit money from Jack's estate.'

This had occurred to Luke but he would never mention it. Trust Crystal to only care about the money.

'I didn't ask her to call,' he protested.

'Don't worry. I know what Crystal's like. Anyhow, Megan's death changes nothing. The way your father wrote the will, you get whatever's left in your college fund when you graduate, plus a few thousand more. It's a male thing, Luke. He thought you needed to make your own way in the world.'

Luke wanted to say something about Megan, but couldn't, not with her standing right by him.

'I'm not about money,' Luke told his uncle.

'If you say so, Luke. Jack thought that Megan would do whatever she wanted regardless of how much money she had. He wasn't sure the same was true of you.'

Which may be right, but the truth hurt, and Luke couldn't resist an impulse to stab at Uncle Mike in return.

'And what do you get in the will if the body in the Barbican turns out to be Megan?' It was a direct question that an adult would never ask. Luke didn't care. Megan, at his side, leaned closer so that she could hear the answer.

'I don't want to get into that at the moment, Luke. We should be focusing on finding your sister's killer and making sure you're safe. Where are you?'

'I'm in Brooklyn, staying at a friend's.'

'OK, you're probably safe there for the time being,' Mike said, 'provided you lay low and don't tell anyone else where you are. I gather your mother's renting a place in the Village. Let me check out the security before you move in with her. If there is a threat, you could be more vulnerable in Manhattan. I've got an urgent call on another line. Hang tough, kid.'

That was something Mike always used to say, reminding Luke that his uncle had been around all his life, far more than his own father had.

'Wait. There's something else,' he started to say, but Mike had already hung up.

'What the hell?' his sister asked as soon as the call finished. 'I thought you were going to tell him about me and hand over the phone?'

'I didn't get a chance.' Luke summed up the discussion. 'I wanted to tell him about you but he hung up too soon. I'm sorry. I didn't know how to handle it. A couple of times, Mike spoke about you in the present tense, as though he hoped you really were alive. It didn't feel right.'

'What do you mean, *didn't feel right*? You're getting really paranoid, Luke. Call him back.'

'Let's leave it a while. He was taking an urgent call.'

Ten minutes later, when Luke called, Mike had just left for an urgent meeting. He had a lot going on.

Fourteen

Megan and Luke sat down to watch the early evening news. She'd only been dead for a day, but Megan had already faded from the headlines. Life went on without you. She had learned that early, when Mum died. Now she was having to learn it all over again. Dad's death was still making waves but the ocean had closed up around her in seconds. She felt dreadfully alone.

There was a crashing noise in the hall. Megan swore and shot out of her chair. 'Someone's breaking in!'

'Don't panic,' Luke said. 'It's only Andy.'

'Is he expecting me?' They should have discussed this, but hadn't.

'I told him I had a girl coming. Best if he doesn't know who you are.'

'Won't he recognize me?'

'The picture on the news looked nothing like you. I'll tell him you're visiting from England. What's your name?'

Andy walked in, a long-haired kid Luke's age, carrying a skateboard. Too late to come up with a name.

'Wassup?' he said.

'Nothin' much,' Luke said. 'Andy, this is the friend I was telling you about. She's over from England and I persuaded her to split from her parents for a few days. Meet Ginger.'

Megan winced. *Ginger?*

'Ginger, huh? I guess your parents took one look at you and thought, naming her's going to be easy.'

'Actually,' Megan fibbed, 'I was blonde when I was a baby. I was nicknamed "Ginger" because my mum's a huge fan of Ginger Rogers. Heard of her? She used to dance with Fred Astaire?'

Andy looked bemused. He wasn't sure if Megan was teasing him, so played it straight. 'Whatever. You're welcome to stay, Ginger. Here on your own?'

'I'm afraid so. I've just been comforting poor Luke here on what happened to his sister.'

Andy nodded sagely. 'Tragic. Did you know her?'

'Met her once,' Megan improvised. 'We got on but she was a couple of years older than me. So, you know, we weren't going to become bosom buddies.'

If Andy thought Megan looked older than Luke, he didn't let on. They made small talk for a few minutes, then Andy went for a shower. Megan looked at her watch. It was after six. Just after eleven in Scotland. Megan needed to talk to Grace and the ward would be quiet. Her friend might not be awake but . . .

'Want to do it now?' Luke asked, handing her his phone.

Megan nodded. 'What are you going to say?'

She dialled the number. When it began to ring, she handed the phone back to Luke. She listened to her brother make the introduction. He did it pretty well, she thought.

'Grace? This is Luke, Megan's brother . . . Thanks, but there's no need for condolences, that's why I'm calling.

Before I explain, are you alone? OK, here's the thing. Megan escaped. That was somebody else's body they found. And she's sitting with me right now. It's a shock, I know. Are you OK? Sure? I'm going to hand the phone over to her right now.'

It was such a relief to hear Grace's voice that Megan began to cry. Her friend was crying too.

'I was so upset, Megan. I've been in torment. My mum wants an armed guard at the hospital because she's afraid somebody will have another go at killing me.'

'It can't have been you they were after, Grace. It must have been me.'

'That's what I told Mum. But why?'

'Something to do with the reason Dad was killed, probably.'

'What are you going to do?'

'I don't know. Apart from you and Luke, I don't know who to trust. You two are the only ones who know I'm here, and I want to keep it that way.'

'What about your uncle?'

'I . . . I tried to go and see him this morning, but they wouldn't let me into the office. Things are a bit crazy at the company at the moment. I'm sure he'll help but . . . he doesn't know that I'm alive. Maybe the fewer people who know, the safer I am.'

She and Grace tossed ideas around for a few minutes but didn't get far. Andy had a huge sofa covered by an old grey blanket. Luke sat on its edge, picking holes in the blanket.

'Either it's terrorists or somebody who doesn't want you and Luke to take over Kite Industries,' Grace concluded.

'I guess,' Megan replied.

'If you don't make it to your eighteenth birthday, who stands to benefit?' Grace asked, getting to the nub of things.

'I don't know. Neither Luke nor I were at the will reading. Not that there's going to be a great deal to inherit if things keep falling apart the way they have been doing.'

'Stock prices always go up and down, Megan. They're like poker chips, not real money. Kite makes loads of popular software. That's not going to change.'

'I suppose.'

'Do you want me to try and see what was in the will?'

'If you can do it without people finding out I'm alive.'

'I'll find out somehow. But listen. It's hard to stay hidden for long. There are so many ways to trace people. You need to be very careful.'

'I'm using Luke's phone,' Megan explained. 'An American mobile. Also, I haven't used my cards in the US. In fact, I couldn't.'

'They've been cancelled because you're dead?'

'Maybe, but that's the other thing I needed to tell you.'

She explained how, in her hurry, she had taken Grace's passport and credit card. This amused Grace.

'If you're me, that means you're already over eighteen and a legal adult. Congratulations. You should be fine as long as nobody works out that you're also stuck in an Edinburgh hospital with two broken legs.'

Grace told her what the card's credit limit was. £2,000.

'I've got your cash card too. Do you know how much money there is in your account?'

'Not much. A few hundred.'

A tiny amount, by Megan's standards, but it would come in useful.

'Buy yourself a new SIM card for your phone, then you can call me without using your brother's phone.'

'Good idea. When's the best time?'

'Around now is good, or at lunchtime between one and two, before visiting hours start. I'll sleep with the phone under my pillow, set on "vibrate".'

'You're a star,' Megan said.

'I could talk to my mum. She might be able to help.'

'Not while I'm in the US,' Megan said. 'Until I sort out what's going on it's best if the whole world thinks I'm dead.'

Megan told Luke about the call, then felt very tired. She was jetlagged and not fully over her illness. She lay down on the sofa to have a nap.

When she woke, Luke was reading one of Andy's comics.

'Have you seen my phone?' he asked her.

'No,' said Megan, 'but I had it earlier. It must be around. I'd be safe to use mine if I put in a new SIM card.'

'Want me to get one now?'

'That'd be cool.'

'I won't be long.'

While Luke was out, Andy came back.

'Your boyfriend left you on your own?'

'He's not my boyfriend.'

Andy grinned. 'Oh . . . I'm in with a chance, then?'

'I prefer older guys.'

'Good escape.' He smiled. 'Where are your parents?'

'Sorry?' Megan didn't know what lie Luke had told.

'Luke said you'd managed to dump them for a few days.'

'Oh. Yeah. They're doing, y'know, culture. A play on Broadway. Lots of museums and art galleries. A yawn.'

'You think? I kind of like some of that stuff.'

'Me too. Some. But only in small doses.'

'You prefer shopping?'

Megan shook her head. 'How many pairs of jeans or shoes do you need? I like to travel light. I've got a camera and music on my phone, a couple of audiobooks. Why do I need more?'

'So what do you plan to do while you're here?'

'I like to explore places on foot or on a bike. That's my thing.'

'I've got an old racer you can borrow, if you like.'

'Really? That would be brilliant.'

'It's in the basement. Help yourself. Say, would you like to see my comic book collection?'

What was it with boys and comic books? But Megan knew when to be diplomatic. 'Go on. As long as you get dressed first.'

'Give me five minutes.'

While Andy was out of the room, Megan worked out where Luke's mobile must have gone. She pulled the blanket off the sofa. She could see why Andy's parents had covered it. The sofa was mottled with unsavoury stains, tears and cigarette burns. There, sure enough, was Luke's phone. He had a new text. They had no secrets, she figured. So she read the message.

Fifteen

There was a store on Fourth Avenue that sold SIM cards cheaply. Luke cycled down Union St, glad to be out of Andy's house, happy to feel the wind on his face. His route took him past Kal's place. Luke wondered how his friend was doing. He wouldn't have glanced down Kal's street had it not been for the sirens. They were loud, insistent and getting nearer.

Luke pressed hard on his brakes but still overshot the turning. The sirens cut off, one by one, as the ambulance and fire engines arrived at their destination. Luke dismounted and dragged his bike on to the pavement. When the 'walk' signal flashed, he crossed Union to Kal's street.

Whatever had happened was bad. Police were taping off the road. Medics carried a stretcher into one of the brownstone houses. Kal's house. But Kal was away. Luke wheeled his bike nearer the house, to see what was going on. A few neighbours were out in the street. There was one young woman who Luke recognized. He had met her at Kal's house. She was holding a toddler. He introduced himself as a friend of Kal's.

'What's going on here?'

'The house was attacked. I heard them break in. A lot of

shouting. I called the police but the intruders were gone before they got here.'

'A burglary?'

The neighbour shook her head. 'They weren't carrying anything when they left. But I heard shots.'

'What kind of guys were they?'

'White. My age. Scarves around their faces but not a gang look. More like a disguise. I don't think Kal would have been home. He's at Cape Cod with his father. His big sister, Maria, she babysits for me sometimes. She was home.'

Luke pictured Maria. Tall, slim, dirty blonde, nineteen, just finished her first year at college.

'Oh no,' the neighbour said, and seemed to stagger. Luke had never understood the phrase 'weak at the knees' until now. He caught her. The woman rested her head on his shoulder and began to weep. The medics carried the stretcher out in the bright, June sun. The body they were carrying was covered. A few strands of blonde hair hung loose beneath the plastic. His friend's sister was dead.

The street's onlookers stood in uneasy silence.

'Looks like she was home alone,' Luke heard one of the police say. 'Two shots to the head. A military-style operation.'

'I'm sorry,' Luke told the crying woman. 'I've got to go.'

He got on his bike and hurried uphill, back to his sister. It was her the killers were after, he was sure of that. They thought he was living with Kal. Somehow, the intruders had discovered that Megan was alive and worked out that she must be with him. How long before they found where she really was?

Luke got back to the house less than half an hour after he'd left. Andy was in the living room, reading a comic.

'Where's Ginger?' Luke asked.

His friend shrugged. 'I was talking to her earlier, but when I came down a few minutes ago, she was gone.'

'She didn't say anything about going out?'

'No, sorry, man. Looks like she blew both of us off.'

'Or someone came and got her.'

'You mean her parents? She didn't look the sort to let her parents push her around.'

'You sure she didn't say anything?'

'Not a word.'

'Could anyone have been in the house?'

'Come on!' Andy said. 'She's probably just gone for a walk. Or a bike ride. We were gonna look at my comic collection, but I mentioned she could borrow the bike I keep in the basement.'

Perhaps that was all it was. Megan had gone for a ride to avoid having to discuss comics with Andy. It made sense. At any other time it would have made sense.

Megan rode hard, paying little attention to the traffic. After reading the text, half an hour ago, she'd hauled Andy's bike out of the basement and hit the street. She wore a greasy Brooklyn Dodgers baseball cap to ward off the sun and hide her hair. Now she cycled round the neighbourhood, trying to work out where to go next.

She thought through the events of the last half hour. The message on Luke's phone was unusually grammatical, for a text message. Sent half an hour ago, it said: GET OUT OF THE

HOUSE AT ONCE. DON'T BRING MEGAN. Which was exactly what Luke had done, only Megan wasn't sure how he could have read this message before setting off. Was buying a new card for her phone just an excuse? No. Luke would never leave her alone in a house where she was in danger of dying. And she had been sleeping on top of his phone. He hadn't seen the message.

Somebody else must know that Megan was alive and in the US. But there was only her, Luke and Andy, who had no idea who she really was.

Andy! Was he at risk, too? Megan thought about phoning him. She got out Luke's phone and found his friend's number. Then she felt the phone vibrate. A new text was coming in. She braked, propped the bike against a street light, and read it.

WHERE ARE YOU? COME TO THE NEW PLACE TONIGHT.

The message was followed by a street address and an apartment number. In Manhattan, presumably. Was it Luke's mum? Megan scrolled through the phone's contact list. There was an entry for Crystal but under a different number.

Andy wasn't at risk. She was. Megan had tried hard not to believe it, but the evidence was staring her in the face. When you combined the two messages, it became clear: Luke was part of a conspiracy to kill her. And, therefore, part of the conspiracy that killed her dad.

The rush-hour traffic was building up around her. Megan got back on to Andy's bike. The tyre pressure was dangerously low and it didn't have a lock. Never mind. The thing was so battered that she doubted anyone would steal it.

She had been cycling aimlessly. Now she found herself by the bike store she had passed earlier. She went in and asked if she could borrow a pump. The big black man behind the counter laughed at her.

'You look like a girl who can afford to buy herself a bike pump.'

'Normally, yes, but I haven't had the chance to go to a cash machine.'

'Cash machine. Is that what they call those holes in the wall where you come from? Here, this is my cheapest pump. Previously owned. Steel, so it's heavy, but it does the job.' He handed her a short, black bike pump, priced at ten dollars. 'Pay me for it next time you're passing.'

'Thanks. I appreciate it. I'm Megan.'

'You're welcome, Megan. I'm Dave.'

'Dave, can you tell me where the nearest metro is where I can carry a bike on to the train?'

Outside, Megan pumped up her tyres, then cycled to the subway station Dave had directed her to. Ambulances and police cars hurtled past her, their sirens on. There was always somebody in worse trouble than you were. She should have used Grace's credit card to pay for the pump and bought a lock, too, but she wasn't thinking straight. That was why she'd told Dave her real name.

There was no cash machine outside the metro. Never mind. There would be plenty in Manhattan. With her last two dollars, Megan bought a single to Manhattan and hauled her bike into the subway station. On her back was a knapsack she'd taken from Andy's. She'd filled it in a hurry, but it contained everything she needed, a change of clothes, her memory stick, some toiletries.

Megan didn't know where she'd sleep tonight. Probably her best bet was to ring her uncle, let him know that she was alive, take things from there. If she knew his address, she'd go directly uptown, but all she remembered was that he lived in a penthouse on the Upper West Side. She might recognize the building once she was in the neighbourhood. She might not.

'She just ran out on you, Luke. I hate to say it, but Ginger was too old and too good looking for you, bro'. How old did you say she was?'

'Seventeen.'

'Girls that age want to be with a guy in his twenties. Nineteen, bare minimum.'

'You're probably right. I wish I could find my phone.'

Luke had searched the house from top to bottom but there was no sign of it.

'Maybe Ginger took it,' Andy said. 'She's got my bike. And the little grey knapsack that I use to take my stuff to work.'

It sounded like Megan had left on purpose, rather than been dragged away. That was good. It meant she was safe and it meant that whoever killed Maria didn't know where Luke was. But it didn't explain why Megan had left the house.

Screw it! Luke thought. He needed to speak to Mike. His uncle was the only one who could sort the situation out. He had the UK pay-as-you-go but that didn't work here. Needs must. He turned on Megan's phone. As expected, it worked in the US. Megan always had the best. And Uncle Mike's number was in there. Luke took a deep breath and pressed 'call'. The phone took an age to connect, presumably because it was being routed to the UK and back. When it began to ring, his uncle picked up at once.

'Megan? Is that you?'

Was he expecting this call from a dead girl?

'Megan, talk to me. We have a lot to sort out.'

Something was wrong, Luke decided. Something was very wrong. He hung up.

Sixteen

The address in the text was in Greenwich Village, in the heart of Manhattan island. The house was a short walk from the hotel where Luke had been staying, close to the designer shops that lined the upper end of Bleecker Street, near Abingdon Square. Was this where Crystal was moving to? Megan cycled along Eighth Avenue and turned on to the narrow street named in the text. The message told Luke to come tonight. It was barely seven. He wouldn't be expected yet.

The tall buildings had railings at the front. An old bike lock was tied to the railings of one of the shabbier houses. There was no bike attached to it. Megan wrapped the chain round Andy's bike to give the impression that it was locked. Nobody would go to any effort to steal a bike as old and knocked about as this one.

The building in the text was what Americans called a condominium. That is, it was divided into flats. The apartment Megan was after had a 2 in front of it. In the US, Megan remembered, ground floor flats were called the first floor, so the 2 meant the first floor up, rather than the second. Megan tried the front door. It was firmly locked and had security buzzers. Megan walked quickly around the front of the building. An old-fashioned black fire escape ran up each side. She decided to go up the left side and see what she could see.

How many second-floor apartments were there? Megan remembered Luke saying that Crystal's apartment faced on to the street, so, if this was her building it had to be the front apartment. Or were there two front ones? The fire escape on the left-hand side led only to a locked door.

Megan hurried down and across the building, then climbed the spiral metal staircase on the building's right. The fire escape on the second floor wasn't entered through a door. It had a large window where the door was on the other side. You would have to smash it to escape. And the window had a vent, which, on this warm evening, was wide open. Megan could hear salsa music coming from inside.

She pressed her body against the window. This side of the building was in shade. She could be noticed from the street, but only if someone were really looking. By leaning in, she could see a spacious living area with wooden floors and empty walls: a sign that the occupant had only just moved in. Megan ducked her head back, not wanting to be seen by whoever was inside.

On the street outside, a car was manoeuvring into the one free parking space. From where she stood, Megan could hear it, but couldn't see anything beyond a narrow strip of road. A minute later, a buzzer sounded and the salsa music was turned off. Megan heard a coarse accent.

'You got away earlier than I was expecting. Come on up.'

The voice was Crystal's. Megan leaned forward to see inside the living room. Now that the music was off, she could hear an air-conditioning unit's constant whirr. Yes, there was Crystal, with her back to Megan. She wore a short skirt and her hair was luxuriously coiffured. She turned to open the door. Seeing Luke's mother in profile, Megan could understand what had attracted her father, nearly seventeen years ago. Crystal was a sexy, pert blonde. The door opened and the man from the intercom came in.

'Are we alone?'

'It's just us, hon,' Crystal said, and swept the man straight into her arms. Megan should have ducked back out of sight, but she couldn't believe what she was seeing. Straining her back to get a good view, she had to wait until they pulled apart to be absolutely sure. It really was him. Crystal was being embraced by Megan's uncle, Mike Kite.

'Where are you off to?'

'Out. Sorry, Andy. I need to find Ginger. Don't wait up.'

'Good luck, but I'm warning you, Kite. I've met her type. That one's a heartbreaker.'

'You could be right there.'

Out on the street, Luke didn't know where to turn. Two girls had been killed by the people who were after Megan. A third was still in the hospital. Had Megan heard about Maria? Was that why she'd left Andy's? Surely it had happened too quickly.

At least Megan had taken Andy's bike, not his. Luke rode to the subway station, his head constantly moving from side to side. No sign of anyone following him. Where to go? His plan had been to talk to Uncle Mike, but the phone call earlier had freaked him out. How did Mike know that Megan was alive?

No point in being paranoid. There would be an explanation. Something simple. For instance, that the body in London had been positively identified as someone else.

Luke heaved his hybrid bike over the barrier and waited for a train. Rush hour was still going on, but not in this direction. Nobody worked in Brooklyn and lived in Manhattan. Luke's stomach made a gurgling noise and he realized that he'd forgotten to eat. Again.

The train arrived. Luke tried to make up his mind which route to take, where to change lines. Before he saw his uncle, there was something he had to find out. Only two people knew that he was supposed to be staying at Kal's: Megan, who didn't know where Kal lived, and his mother. Luke didn't believe that Crystal would kill anybody. She wasn't a killer. She was a gossip. He needed to find out who she'd told.

Luke hadn't written down the new address but that was OK, he could remember the way to the condo, near Abingdon Square. He could find a payphone and call first, to see if she was in. Although, thinking about it, Crystal could be evasive. Better, perhaps, to surprise her.

Seventeen

Megan had good hearing. She could make out most of the conversation, except when the couple lowered their voices or there was loud traffic outside. After their first embrace, Crystal and Mike talked about something that had happened in Brooklyn. Megan heard the word 'dead'.

'Have you spoken to Luke?' Mike asked.

Crystal didn't reply directly. Maybe she was shaking her head. Megan daren't look into the room as there was a fair chance that Mike would spot her.

'I could call him now,' Crystal said.

Megan swore beneath her breath. She had Luke's phone in her pocket. If it rang, the couple inside would hear. Crystal would have Luke on speed dial. The call would only take a moment to come through. Megan got the phone out, but, at first glance, couldn't work out how to turn it off. Was it that red button there? She pressed it. Too late. There was a symbol for an incoming call. Quickly, Megan clicked on a left-hand button, which she hoped meant 'ignore'. Crystal's name appeared on the display, with 'call not accepted'. The phone did not ring.

'He's not answering my call,' she heard Crystal say.

'Maybe he's on his way over here,' Mike told her. 'Did . . .'

A car passed and Megan lost a couple of exchanges.

'What I want to know,' Crystal said next, 'is how you're so sure that Megan is alive and in the US.'

'We know she's alive because the girl who was killed in the Barbican wasn't her,' Mike said. 'She was a teenager visiting her grandparents on the floor below Jack's penthouse. The family have been persuaded to keep her death quiet. They were told it's essential for the assassins to think that Megan is dead, so they won't attack her again.'

'That doesn't explain why you're sure she's in New York?'

'This afternoon I saw CCTV footage taken outside the Kite building just after nine this morning. Somebody who looked a lot like Megan came to the Kite offices, asking to see me. Said she *was* Megan, but the receptionist thought a tourist was playing some sick, British joke. The girl left. You don't know anything about that, do you?'

'No. Of course not. Why would I?'

'Because, in the same footage, I saw the girl who looked like my niece hooked up with a guy who, from a distance, was the spitting image of *our* Luke. That sounds like too big a coincidence to me.'

'Luke's with Megan?'

'I think so, but don't know where. He's not staying with . . .'

The buzzer sounded. The voice was distorted so Megan couldn't tell who it was.

'Now we should get some answers,' Crystal said, then threw herself into a hug with Mike, wrapping her arms around him. He embraced her for a moment, then pushed her away.

'Let me take the lead,' he said.

There was a knock on the door. Megan heard a familiar voice.

'Luke!' her uncle said. 'It's great to see you at last! We have a lot to talk about.'

'We sure do,' Luke said.

Megan covered her mouth with her hand to stop herself from throwing up. It was worse than she'd feared. There was a conspiracy against her and they were all in it together.

'First things first,' Mike said. 'Do you know where Megan is?'

'Isn't she here with you?' Luke asked.

Megan got a terrible falling feeling.

'Why would she be?' Crystal wanted to know.

'Because the bike she borrowed is parked right outside this building.'

PART TWO

Eighteen

BROOKLYN

Andy straightened his tie.

'I've never been to the funeral of someone our age before.'

'Me neither,' Luke said.

'Think she knew it was coming?'

Luke thought about this for a moment, remembering everything that had happened in the previous two weeks: the deaths, the 'accidents', the threatening messages. He tried not to think about the gun, the shots to the head.

'I hope not,' was all he said in reply.

'She'd be proud of the way you look today. You're one sharp dude.'

'Am I?' Luke said, looking in the mirror. He'd never worn a suit before and, with his new hair-cut, he felt transformed.

'Look at us. We could be the Blues Brothers!'

A horn sounded outside.

'Car's here,' Andy said. 'Hey, that's a sweet ride. What is it, an Audi? Can you afford that?'

'Don't worry. My uncle's paying.'

The two young men left the house and got into the back seat of the spacious saloon.

'The Green Wood cemetery,' Luke told the driver.

'Of course, sir.'

'Just think,' Andy said, 'she's going to be buried alongside Leonard Bernstein and Joey Gallo. Is that cool, or what?'

'It's kinda cool,' Luke replied. 'But I have a feeling she'd rather still be alive.'

CHICAGO

'You're good to go, Miss Thompson,' said the guy at the ticket desk. 'Your flight leaves in ninety minutes. Check-in closes in forty-five minutes.'

'Thanks.' She had paid extra for a direct flight, rather than change in Munich, Vienna or Toronto. Her plane would get in at half past twelve tomorrow afternoon, European time. By nine US time, when most Americans arrive at work, she would have disappeared into the city, leaving no trace.

All she had to do now was get through Customs. Megan had done it before, arriving in the US, but she had a nasty feeling today would be trickier. Luke had overheard her talking to Grace. He may have worked out that she'd travelled here on Grace's passport. If he had told Uncle Mike and Mike had alerted Homeland Security, Megan could be in trouble.

How to handle the situation if she were caught? Beg for mercy or ask for protection? Would they believe her if she told the truth? Or would they return Megan to her only living adult relative? Her uncle had taken US citizenship.

This was his country, not hers. And he had powerful friends.

No point in hanging around. She would be safer airside than in Departures. Megan joined the queue to check in.

All of the other people in the queue looked Polish. Or maybe they were Chicagoans. Megan didn't know the city or its people. She had only arrived at the airport this morning. After running away from Crystal's flat, she'd taken the subway to Queens, then got on a bus to Cleveland, where she'd stayed in a cheap motel. Yesterday she'd caught a bus to Chicago.

'You have no baggage?' asked the woman at check-in.

'That's right. I'm travelling light,' Megan said.

'Your flight should be ready to board in fifty minutes.'

Megan took her boarding card and headed straight for Customs. This was the tricky bit. When the Customs officer put her UK passport through his scanner, an alarm might go off. Trembling, she avoided the officer's eyes and handed over the passport. Soon, there'd be facial recognition software and she'd have no chance. But not yet. The officer gave Megan one glance and decided that she sufficiently resembled the photograph.

At the baggage X-ray she was made to take off her shoes and her belt. Every little thing she owned went through the X-ray machine. Still, there was no alarm. She tucked Grace's passport and her boarding card back into her jacket, then put her shoes back on. Megan had to give an index-finger fingerprint, but that should be nothing to worry about. It would match the fingerprint she had given on entering the county.

At last, she was airside.

BROOKLYN

'Thanks for coming, Luke, I appreciate it.'

Luke wrapped an arm around his friend's shoulder.

'Anything I can do? It's such a tough time.'

'You can tell me what it's like, living without a big sister,' Kal said. 'All my life, there was Maria, bossing me around, looking after me. Now there's just me, the only son. How do you deal with that?'

'I don't know,' Luke said. Behind them, mourners began to get into cars and leave the leafy cemetery. 'I haven't come to terms with any of what's happened.'

'I'm sorry, I forgot. You haven't buried Megan yet. What kind of world is this turning into, Luke, when both our sisters get shot down for no reason? They didn't take a thing from the house. Not one thing. What could anyone have against Maria?'

'Mistaken identity is all I can think,' Luke mumbled.

'That's what the police say, that it was a gang thing. But what gangs work round our part of town? Makes no sense.'

The two young men hugged, then Kal joined his parents for the long drive home. Luke returned to his chauffeured car.

'That looked . . . emotional,' Andy said.

'I can't begin to tell you,' Luke replied. He wished he could tell Andy how guilty he was feeling, how he was increasingly sure that a few loose words of his had led to Maria's death.

'Are you coming back to mine, or going to your mom's in

Manhattan?' Andy wanted to know.

'I think I'd better go to Mom's for a couple of days. But if it's OK, I'll crash at yours again soon.'

'Sure. My folks are away for another six weeks.'

They stopped to drop Andy. Luke went in to collect some of his stuff.

'Did that girl ever show up?' Andy asked him. 'What was her name: Ginger? That was a made-up name, right?'

'Yeah. I think it was made up,' Luke admitted. 'She never told me her real name. I guess she went back to her parents', flew home. I never heard from her again.'

'She still owes me a bike and a knapsack.'

'She owes me a phone,' Luke said. 'Listen, you can have my bike. I hardly ever use it.'

'I never used mine. It sucked. But thanks for the offer.'

'I'll leave the bike here anyway. See you soon.'

His uncle's car service took him over Brooklyn Bridge and into Manhattan. Most of the traffic was going the other way. Nevertheless, the journey was slow. Luke had plenty of time to think about the events of the last few days, since Maria was shot and Megan disappeared.

Had he imagined Andy's bike outside Mom's new flat? It wasn't there when Uncle Mike and he hurried out to find her. Then he'd had a lot of explaining to do. Every word of that uncomfortable conversation was etched into his memory:

'You knew your sister was alive and didn't tell me?'

'It was for Megan to tell you, Mike.'

'And why didn't she?'

'She tried. She turned up at your office yesterday morning

115

and was sent away. That's when I met her. I was coming to see you.'

'And you took her back to Brooklyn? Why?'

Luke had no easy answer for this. Crystal was standing behind Mike. He couldn't explain that he didn't trust his mom.

'Someone nearly killed her in London. Megan wanted to be in an obscure place, one where nobody expected her to be.'

'Then why did she come here tonight?' Crystal asked.

'You tell me. I went out to get a SIM card for her phone and when I got back she was gone.'

Luke decided not to mention the death of Kal's sister. He wanted to know if his uncle or mother already knew about it.

'What happened to your phone?' Mom asked. 'I tried to call you.'

'I think Megan has it.'

'How did she get into the country anyway?' Mike wanted to know.

'She caught a plane,' Luke said. He wasn't sure how she managed to get in unnoticed. 'Look, what's going on? Why are people trying to kill me and Megan?'

'Nobody's trying to kill you,' Mom said. 'What happened to our apartment was an accident. The gas authority's taken responsibility.'

'Good,' Luke said. Kal was always quoting this guy who said there was no such thing as a coincidence. Luke wished he could remember his name. Bill something. 'Perhaps you can explain. Why is someone trying to kill Megan, but not me?'

'Megan's effectively the owner of Kite Industries,' Mike said. 'She's one of the richest young people in the world.

116

Maybe the richest. In a position like that, you can't count your enemies.'

'Where do you think she's gone?' Crystal asked Luke. 'Back to where you were staying?'

'Where have *you* been staying?' Mike asked.

'With a friend.'

'Kal?' Crystal asked.

'No, turned out Kal was out of town. Look, just a friend. I'm sixteen now. I can have some privacy when I choose.'

'Of course you can,' Mike said. 'It's just that we're very concerned about Megan.'

'Me too,' Luke said. 'Shouldn't we call the police?'

Curiously, neither his uncle nor his mother had seemed very keen on that idea.

Nineteen

KRAKOW, POLAND

The airport was smaller than Megan was used to. You had to walk from the plane to Arrivals rather than take a bus. Megan was anxious to get away. There were ten or eleven people in each of the four immigration queues. For some reason, hers was slower than the rest.

When there were fewer than a dozen people left, Megan's queue ground to a halt. She'd clearly chosen the line with the pickiest officer. He was minutely examining a middle-aged man's laptop. Trying not to look nervous, Megan read and reread the rubric at the front of Grace's passport: *Her Britannic Majesty's Secretary of State requests and requires in the Name of Her Majesty all those whom it may concern to allow the bearer to pass freely without let or hindrance, and to afford the bearer such assistance and protection as may be necessary.* Fancy words, but they probably weren't much use when you were travelling with borrowed documents.

A woman soldier in grey uniform stepped forward and spoke rapid Polish to Megan. Was she in trouble? No. Megan realized that she was being told to move to another of the roped-off lines, one where there was no longer a queue. The immigration officer at this booth smiled at her, took the shortest of glances at her passport, ran it through a card reader, then waved her through. Megan entered Poland.

Megan no longer had the carry-on bag she'd taken to the States, just the little grey knapsack that belonged to Andy. She had no fancy shoes or make-up, only a few toiletries, a short dress, two changes of underwear and the clothes she was standing in.

Once she got through Customs, Megan changed her remaining dollars into zlotys. According to the in-flight magazine, Krakow airport was a short ride to the city, so she decided to take a cab rather than wait for a bus.

'How much to the city?' she asked.

'Eighty zloty.'

'OK. Can you take me to a cheap, quiet hotel?'

'Hotel? OK.'

She wasn't sure that the driver had understood the 'cheap, quiet' bit, but once she was in the right area, Megan could scout around until she found somewhere suitable. She checked the exchange rate and realised that the cab fare into the city was about the same as a ride from midtown Manhattan to JFK. Nearly fifty precious dollars. Never mind. The taxi took a bridge over a crowded motorway and continued on a single-lane road, passing quaintly shaped buildings that reminded her of folk tales she'd been told in primary school.

After a few kilometres, the cab was forced to slow down. Cars were queuing to overtake a vehicle that seemed to be moving at a snail's pace. Only when they overtook it did Megan realize what it was: two men driving a horse and cart.

This was another world. Surely nobody would find her here.

As they passed the cart, something moved in the back. Instinctively, Megan ducked. The taxi driver gave her a confused look. As well he might, for now the moving creature raised its head. Not a concealed assassin. A black goat.

The taxi drove into the south side of the city. They passed a rundown funfair, then crossed a bridge over the river that ran round Krakow. On a hill to the left was a large castle. The city was old fashioned, not the monochrome ex-Soviet stronghold she'd expected when she booked the flight. According to the in-flight magazine, Krakow was the first place the Nazis invaded in the Second World War. It wasn't bombed by either side, so all of its old architecture remained intact.

The taxi driver dropped her at a Best Western hotel. Should she go somewhere cheaper? Maybe, but it would need to be a place that took credit cards. Megan presented herself at Reception.

'I'm sorry, we're fully booked.'

'Oh. Right. Do you know anywhere that—'

'This is the height of the season, so you'll be lucky, but . . .' The woman pointed at a pile of copies of a free, slim, softback guide to the city. There were a bunch of free maps, too. Megan snaffled one and returned to the street. Her taxi was already gone. Megan pored over the map. The street she was on, Starowisina, led straight into the centre, so she followed it. Old-fashioned trams kept passing, each one crammed with people, but the distance didn't look too far to go by foot. The shops got smarter the further in she went, but it was hardly Oxford St. Plaster peeled from the walls of some of the buildings.

Megan asked about rooms in two hotels, but each was full. She'd chosen Krakow because it was remote and she'd thought that the former Russian bloc countries were unpopular. Wasn't the UK full of Poles who wanted to escape their own country?

Megan passed an internet café, then a stylish sushi bar that could have easily been in London's West End or Manhattan. The world was shrinking, she thought. Nowhere was remote any more. You could get anything anywhere. She had decided on Krakow almost at random: the city was one of the few places she could get a flight to that had no Kite Industries office. It was as good a place to hide as any. Before she picked a hotel, she ought to see if she could pick up a SIM card for Luke's phone. She wanted to be able to make calls that were completely untraceable.

A thin band of green park ran round the very centre of the city. Megan turned down Sienna. At the end of this pretty street she found herself in a vast square, the biggest she had ever seen, with a long building at the centre. Fancy stores and restaurants lined the sides. Her SIM card proved easy to find. She bought one for twenty zloty in the Empik Media Store. The guy who sold it to her also gave Megan a lead on a hotel. 'Not too expensive but a little way out.' He put an X on her map. He flicked through her guidebook for her. 'Here. Look.'

'Thanks a lot.'

'Come here again. Tell me if you like it. We have nice internet café and lots of books. You enjoy. My name Tomas.'

He was hitting on her. She smiled. 'Thanks. I'm Grace.'

Megan sat at a shaded table outside an old Polish restaurant. After a few minutes, she was glad she'd chosen to sit back from the edge of the tables. The customers at the front had a better view of the market square but were bugged by panhandlers and flower sellers. Megan didn't want attention. She wore sunglasses and had most of her hair stuffed into a baseball cap. Maybe she should dye her hair, too, to be on the safe side. The red tinge in her hair made her conspicuous. Only one or two people in a hundred had it. But she was meant to be dead. Why would anybody look for her here?

A waitress came and Megan ordered a plate of *pirogi*, little dumplings stuffed with cabbage. Then she got out Luke's phone and put in the new SIM card, which should make it untraceable. How many minutes of international time would her twenty zlotys buy her? In the UK, the evening visiting hours at the hospital had just begun. It would not be safe to ring Grace until tomorrow.

Megan's body clock said it was lunchtime but it was already early evening in Krakow. She needed somewhere to sleep. While waiting for her dumplings, she turned on the phone, which welcomed her to Poland. Megan tapped in the number that the cute guy in Empik had found for her.

MANHATTAN

Where was Megan? Luke was beginning to suspect the worst. He'd been all over Manhattan, looking for her. On the third day of this search, he found what he thought was

Andy's bike. The rust-bucket was unlocked and abandoned in an alley off Broadway in the Upper West Side. He rode it around, showing pictures of his sister to people on the street, in stores and cafés, asking if they'd seen her. None had. Only one recognized her.

'She's that rich dead girl, isn't she? I saw her picture on the news. What are you doin', showing her picture around?'

Luke rode Andy's bike back to his mom's new apartment.

'Where did you get that?' Crystal asked. 'What happened to the beautiful bike your father bought you?'

'It's at . . .' Luke stopped himself from saying 'Andy's'. He didn't want to draw his friend into this, or reveal to Crystal where he stayed when he wasn't with her. So he lied.

'It's being repaired. New chain and wheel straightening. I'm going to Brooklyn to pick it up tomorrow. The guy at the store lent me this until he'd done the job.'

'I knew they did loaners with cars but I've never heard of it with bicycles before.'

'It's a good store,' Luke said. 'What's for dinner?'

'I'm having dinner out, with a friend. Eat whatever you can find, or order in pizza. I'll leave you some cash.'

Mom went to get changed. Luke wondered who she was going out with. He knew better than to ask. It was useful she had a date. With Crystal absent, he could turn this place over.

Twenty

KRAKOW

On her way to the hotel that Tomas had recommended, Megan stopped in a department store and bought herself a pair of cotton shorts. They were cheap and unflattering but would keep her cooler in this hot city. The back street hotel was basic but took credit cards, provided breakfast and had the internet for guests' use. Megan waited until gone midnight to get on it.

The connection was slow. When Megan finally got in to her webmail there were over a hundred emails to go through. Most were spam that had defeated the filters. Many were newsletters she'd signed up for. She might read some of those later. There were several from school-friends, some quite recent. When Megan opened them, she wished she hadn't.

To whoever's opening Megan's email, please accept my condolences Celia had written. *Megan and I were big buddies and I can't believe what has happened. Please would you send me details of her funeral as I would like to attend.*

All of the emails from friends were heartbreaking. Megan felt guilty for putting her friends through such a dreadful deception. She couldn't bring herself to read them through and kept clicking 'next'.

Seventy messages in, one appeared that confused her. She didn't recognize the address. It appeared to come from Japan. But it didn't look like spam. The message was addressed to her personally.

> *Dear Megan*
> *I can't begin to imagine what you're going through, but if you're still alive to open this, things aren't as bad as they must seem. The important thing is to stay hidden until your eighteenth birthday. Trust nobody, not even the police. Blood is no protection. Please reply to this to let me know you're alive, then delete this message and your reply, then empty the deleted items folder. You never know when somebody may be looking.*
> *A friend*

Weird. The only friend who knew that Megan was alive was Grace. She was still in hospital, with no computer. Megan had texted her earlier: SAFE. WILL RING TMROW. So who was this 'friend'? It could be Luke, or their uncle. But in *Japan*? And it didn't sound like either of them. Megan made a note of the email address she was writing to then did as the email asked. She double deleted both the message and her four word reply. *Safe. Who are you?*

Did somebody else have access to her email? The friends who emailed her had assumed as much, but Megan had given her password to nobody. Getting in to an email account should take a court order. But maybe all that went by the board when you died. Maybe you lost all of your privacy.

She read the news online and searched for stories about

125

herself and her uncle. There wasn't much. One of the Sundays had done a sob story about her tragic death. It was strewn with quotes from Brunts' girls who hardly knew her. According to them, Megan was sporty, brainy, celibate and did stuff for charity. They made her sound incredibly boring. Nobody criticized Megan for being snooty, shallow, self-centred, cliquey and annoyingly rich. These were all things she thought about herself, in her darker moments. Megan hadn't made firm arrangements, but she had planned to work in a village in Africa just as Grace's brother, Ethan, was doing. She'd had little fancies about meeting someone like Ethan while she was in Africa, someone who'd see her as she was, without the dollar signs flashing in front of her. Megan needed to experience real life before she went to university. She had been due to leave the day after her eighteenth birthday. Now, instead of the Africa experience, she was getting the run-for-your-life experience.

Tomorrow, Megan decided, after she'd spoken to Grace, she'd do some touristy stuff, try to unwind. She would withdraw some cash. A hotel was OK in the short term but Grace's card had a much lower credit limit than hers. Megan would need to find a job and somewhere cheaper to live. With a UK passport, she should be OK to work in Poland. Waitressing, shop work, whatever. Maybe Tomas from Empik could help her.

MANHATTAN

The rental papers were easy to find, in the same folder where

Mom kept her unpaid bills and legal letters. The letters were mostly from the accountant who handled the maintenance payments from Dad. Luke noted that the latest letter said that, in the light of Jack Kite's death, there would be no further monthly payments. Predictable, but Mom hadn't mentioned this to Luke.

The lease contained no surprises. This place was in Crystal's name, but she had a guarantor. Uncle Mike. Luke could have predicted this, too. Uncle Mike was his godfather and he had always got on with Crystal better than his brother had.

Suppose it was more than that? Could Mike or Crystal be behind the attacks on Megan? Luke couldn't understand why they would be, unless there was something about Dad's will that he hadn't been told.

There was another possibility, that the two of them had something sexual going on. But Luke didn't buy that. Mike had known Mom for as long as Luke was alive. If something were going to happen it would have happened long ago. True, Crystal was looking better than she had for years, though some of her better features verged on the synthetic. No, forget that: Crystal wasn't Mike's type. He tended to date Latino women.

Luke went through the rest of the drawers, hoping to find a copy of his father's will. It wasn't there. Luke featured in the will, so surely he should be able to get hold of a copy. But how?

The buzzer sounded and Luke pressed a button on the intercom. 'Hello?'

'Brooklyn Police Department. Is that Luke Kite?'

'That's me, yes.'

'Luke, we have a few questions for you about the murder

127

of Maria Delgado five days ago. Can we come in?'

'Yes, of course.'

The officers showed Luke their ID at the door. One was a sergeant, the other a detective. Luke wasn't sure how to behave. He desperately wanted to help them find whoever killed Maria. How much should he tell them? That he suspected his mom and/or uncle of involvement? He couldn't. That Megan was still alive? The secret wasn't his to tell and could put his sister in jeopardy. Yet, without knowing about Megan, Maria's killing made no sense. He showed the officers through to the living area.

'How well did you know Maria?' the older officer asked.

'Since I met her brother, Kal, in sixth grade, so, uh, five years or so.'

'And what was your relationship with her?'

'She was my best friend's big sister. We didn't have, like, a *relationship*.'

'But you two got along?'

'Sure. She was nice.'

'Did you know that she was living at her parents' house on her own this summer?'

'No. I knew that Kal was away, so I hadn't been around.'

'I see. And where were you the afternoon that she was murdered?'

'In Brooklyn, visiting a friend.'

'Where exactly in Brooklyn?'

Reluctantly, Luke gave them Andy's address.

'And this friend will confirm that you were with him at the time of Maria's death.'

'Not exactly,' Luke said. 'I think he was in the shower

when I went out.'

If possible, he had to avoid giving them a reason to question Andy, who was bound to mention 'Ginger'.

The younger one took over the questions. 'You went out?'

'On my bike, yes.'

'What for?'

'To . . . um, go to a store.'

'To buy what?'

'I don't remember.'

'I see. And what route did you take?'

'I went down Union, past Kal's street. Of course I heard the sirens.'

'So you don't deny that you were there?'

'No, I saw them bring the body out. I spoke to one of the neighbours.'

'But your being there was a complete coincidence?'

'Yes, of course.'

The two men exchanged glances. 'Where is your bike?' the older one asked.

'At my friend Andy's.'

'What about the clothes you were wearing on the day?'

'I . . . um . . . brought them back here to wash. I guess they're in that laundry basket over there.'

'So you have any objection if we take them for examination?'

'No, but, what is this?' Luke asked. 'What am I suspected of doing?'

The older one's voice became more authoritative, stern.

'Luke Kite, I'm arresting you on suspicion of the murder of Maria Delgado.'

Twenty-One

KRAKOW

Megan woke late and nearly missed breakfast. While she waited for her coffee, she spotted a rack with free newspapers. She reached for one.

'Those are, like, a week old,' an American voice warned.

Megan turned and smiled at a blonde girl a little older than her. 'That's OK. I just like to read while I eat breakfast.'

'My brain doesn't turn on until I've had two shots of coffee,' the girl said, picking up a copy of *Hello*. She didn't seem to recognize Megan, who had her hair tied back but wasn't wearing the baseball cap. She would have felt stupid with it on inside.

Megan hadn't read a paper for ages. These were from the day before she left the States. Neither the *Daily Telegraph* nor the *New York Times* had stories about the Kite family. The only piece with any bearing on Megan's life was a paragraph about a home invasion in Brooklyn. A young woman only a year older than Megan had been shot dead in a quiet street, for no apparent reason. Death, it seemed, was random. Nowhere was safe.

The waitress brought strong coffee. Megan filled up on

bread and jam, then returned to her room. Time to ring Grace. It was an hour earlier in the UK. This was the quiet time at the hospital, after breakfast and doctors' rounds, before visiting began. Megan dialled the number and, after a few seconds, her friend's mobile began to ring.

'Hello?'

'Grace, it's me.'

A pause. 'Simon. Great of you to phone. Can I call you back? I'm in the middle of a thing.'

'OK,' Megan said. 'I'll leave this phone on. Bye.'

Simon was a code word they used when it wasn't cool to talk. It meant her friend wasn't alone and might not have a chance to call for ages. Patience was required.

How to kill time? Megan could look for a job, or a cheaper place to stay. She'd told the hotel she was here for two nights, minimum. She had been warned that they were fully booked at the weekend, three days away. She might as well do some touristy stuff. At least, then, she would blend in. Megan decided to go to the castle, get a feel for the city. Maybe later she'd see Tomas in Empik, see if he knew where a Western European girl could find work in Krakow.

If Megan was going out, she could use some new underwear. It was gross, having to wash her undies in the sink and hang them in the shower to dry. Leaving the room, Megan hesitated. It would be nice to make a proper base for herself but this wasn't it. She had to be ready to run at any time. Megan put her charger, memory stick and ID in her knapsack, together with a change of clothes and the guidebook. The thing felt too heavy to carry round all day. What if she were mugged, lost everything? Better to risk that than having to run and leave everything in her room.

The castle was up a big hill. The grounds were free to get into, although you had to pay if you wanted to go inside the building itself. Next to the castle was a cathedral. No entry fee. Outside the entrance was what the guidebook described as 'dragon's bones'. They were long and kind of convincing. Megan heard an American tourist say they probably came from a dinosaur. Was that what dragons were, dinosaurs? A fading memory of early homo sapiens, easily confused and made into early myth? The thought distracted Megan for at least thirty blissful, almost normal seconds.

The cathedral was crowded but, once inside, most people maintained a respectful silence. It didn't matter if you believed or not, the combination of beauty and spirituality had that effect on people. Megan's family weren't religious, but her mum had had a church funeral and Dad had a religious memorial service. Megan wondered what her own funeral would be like.

She was halfway down the left aisle when her mobile rang. Megan swore to herself and fumbled in the pocket of her shorts. She wasn't used to being embarrassed. It felt like every tourist in the place turned round to shush her or, at the very least, give her angry glances for daring to have her mobile switched on. She pressed 'receive' and whispered: 'Grace, I'm in a church. I can't talk. Just give me a minute to get outside.'

Only the voice at the other end of the phone wasn't Grace.

BROOKLYN

They collected Luke from his cell at 7 a.m. His previous interrogation had ended only six hours before. He'd slept fitfully. Earlier, he'd used his one phone call to ring Uncle Mike's mobile and left a message. They'd let him call his mom, too, but she wasn't picking up either. He kept expecting a lawyer to appear and bail him out. So far, it hadn't happened.

These were different officers from the night before: older. Homicide unit. One wore a cheap ecru suit, the other a black leather blouson, distressed to make it look vintage.

'I want my uncle,' he told the suit.

'You had your phone call last night.'

'You can't hold me like this. I'm only sixteen.'

Leather Jacket sneered. 'This is a capital crime. In this state, you can be tried as an adult when you're sixteen. Go to an adult jail too. But I thought you didn't do anything?'

'No, I didn't!'

'In that case,' the suit said, 'you have nothing to worry about.'

'Tell us where you got the gun,' Leather Jacket said.

'I've never even held a real gun, let alone owned one.'

'You're only making this worse for yourself. We have witnesses who saw you there. You were stupid enough to speak to one of the next-door neighbours.'

'My being there was a coincidence.'

'We don't believe in coincidences,' Leather Jacket said.

'But—'

'There are only lies,' Cheap Suit said, 'and bigger lies.'

133

What could he do to get these guys off his back? Maybe if he told them about Megan, they would understand. But Megan was supposed to be dead. That would only muddy the waters.

'You must have been fond of Maria,' the suit said. 'After all, you went to her funeral.'

'I knew her, but I went to support her brother.'

'We were watching the funeral, you know, seeing who came, videoing the guests. I have to say you had a haunted look about you, Luke. We're trained to recognize that look.'

'It's called *guilt*,' Leather Jacket said.

He was right, that was the worst thing. Luke felt guilty as hell for having inadvertently led Megan's enemies to Maria.

'I was sorry for Kal. I know what it's like to lose a sister.'

'It's OK to admit you were in love with her,' the suit said.

'I wasn't . . .'

'We've all been there. You have feelings for someone who doesn't have feelings back. Or maybe she did but she thought you were too young. So you took the gun over to show her how grown up you were, only things somehow got out of hand . . .'

'No, no.'

Leather Jacket leaned forward. 'You're not getting out of here until we have a confession, Luke. We've got all day.'

Luke closed his eyes. He suddenly felt very tired. He'd read about people making false confessions, just because they got too tired to keep denying it. But until this morning, he'd never understood it. If the stakes were lower, he'd be tempted to confess just to get these jerks off his back.

'I didn't do it,' he said. 'I don't know who did it and if you

134

had a single shred of evidence against me, you'd have charged me by now.'

Bad move. The suit's face hardened and Leather Jacket leaned forward, his grey eyes burning with anger.

'So you want us to charge you?'

Luke could see it coming. They were going to stop playing 'good cop, bad cop' and switch to 'bad cop, evil cop'. Before he could reply, the door opened. A uniform showed in a middle-aged guy who wore an expensively tailored suit with a poorly knotted tie.

'Mr Kite? I'm Marcus Pollack. Your uncle sent me. I'm sorry, I only got the message at seven. Have you been charged?'

Luke shook his head.

'Not yet,' the suit said.

'In that case, I'm taking you home. The police had no right to hold you overnight.'

'We'd like *Mr Kite* to answer a few more questions,' Leather Jacket said.

'I'm sure you would, but given that you've had him in custody for more than ten hours, your chances are nil,' Pollack said. 'Let's get going, Mr Kite.'

Luke followed his lawyer out of the police station.

Twenty-Two

KRAKOW

'So it's true,' said the voice at the other end of the phone. 'You really *are* alive.'

Megan nearly didn't reply. She'd been caught.

'I worked out that *Simon* code last summer. At first, I thought Grace had a serious boyfriend. But then, when you came to stay . . .'

'Yes, Ethan, I'm alive. But Grace and my brother are the only people who know. How did you get hold of her phone?'

'She's having an operation. They're putting a couple of pins in her left leg. She wanted to ring someone first but the doctors wouldn't leave her alone. So she whispered to me. To be honest, I thought it was the anaesthetic talking. Where are you?'

'You really don't want to know.'

'You're right about that.'

'What about you? I thought you were in Namibia.'

'I was, but after what happened to Grace, Mum and Dad started to get a little antsy about my being unprotected out in wildest Africa. Only it wasn't meant to happen to Grace, was it? It was meant to happen to you.'

'I think so, yes.'

'Why is somebody trying to kill you, Megan?'

'I'm not sure. I think it must have something to do with my father, and Kite Industries. I think my brother might be involved. Grace was trying to find out what the contents of my dad's will were, in case they explained everything.'

'You don't know what was in your dad's will? How come?'

'It would take too long to explain. Will you help me?'

'If I can. But I'd better talk to my parents. To Mum, at least. Are you OK with that?'

'I guess . . . but please, the fewer people who know I'm alive, the better. One girl's already been killed.'

'The one they said was you? How have they got away with that?'

'I figure my uncle convinced the victim's family not to contest that the body was mine. He must have told them that would make it easier to find the killer.'

'Megan, are you somewhere safe?'

'I think so. Nobody knows I'm here.'

'How come? There are records whenever anyone travels.'

Megan was silent. Ethan put two and two together.

'You're pretending to be Grace, aren't you? That would explain why the credit card company left a message, checking whether Grace was in Poland. They thought her Visa might have been cloned.'

Megan swore. 'Did you tell them the truth? Have they cancelled the card?'

'Not yet. I tried to ask Grace about the credit card but she was more bothered about the phone call.'

'Listen, Ethan, if you want to help, get Grace to call

them, say she's travelling, increase the credit limit, please.'

'Why? Why can't you come back to the UK?'

'If what my brother told me about Dad's will is half true, I come into my inheritance when I'm eighteen. If I die before then, I'm pretty sure my uncle gets everything.'

'You think your own uncle is behind this? And does he know you're alive?'

'Yes,' Megan said. 'Yes, I'm afraid that he does.'

She had been walking as she talked, and found herself at the edge of the castle grounds, looking over the ramparts. If you paid a few euros, you could take a short cut down a spiral staircase that let you out on to the banks of the river Wisla. The staircase tower was called 'The Dragon's Den'.

'I've got to go, Simon,' Ethan said. 'Mum's just arrived. I need to talk to her. I'll call you later when I've checked that stuff out. If you've got a pen, I'll give you my other number.'

Megan inputted Ethan's mobile number directly into the phone. She walked down the steep, winding stairs that took her out of the castle complex. It was weird, speaking to Ethan again. She had always liked him. Now she had to trust him as well.

At the bottom of the staircase was a dark, wide cave, just about big enough to house a dinosaur. Children gasped but Megan was in no mood to be impressed. She stepped out into bright sunlight to find families posing around a massive metal dragon. As she turned to walk along the river bank, flames shot from its mouth and children cheered. She glanced around her in case she was being followed, but saw only smiling families, couples holding hands, souvenir sellers and a trolley hawking hot dogs and pretzels. She tucked her conspicuous hair more firmly under her shirt and pulled the brim of her baseball cap down, then headed back into the city.

MANHATTAN

'Why didn't you tell me you were there when that girl was murdered?' Mike asked Luke.

'I wasn't there and you never asked about it,' Luke replied.

Marcus Pollack was sitting with Uncle Mike, so Luke could hardly say that he suspected Mike of being involved. They were in the Kite Industries' US headquarters, overlooking Madison Avenue. This was the first time Luke had been in this huge, stylish office, which used to be his father's. He liked it.

'From now on,' Mike said, 'you need to be in a place where your mother and I can keep an eye on you. No more staying with your friend Andy in Brooklyn, OK?'

'OK,' Luke said. He didn't want to put Andy in danger, so that was fine. 'But what about me? Where am I safe?'

'You're not in danger, Luke,' the lawyer said. 'The group that attacked your sister don't seem to have any animus against you, perhaps because it was widely known that Megan was due to inherit Kite Industries on her eighteenth birthday. Until her "death", she was perceived as the rich kid villain. Whereas, in the media, you're still regarded as the unjustly disinherited son.'

Mike nodded. It seemed that he now believed in the

existence of the eco-terrorist group. Luke wasn't so sure.

'You make this sound like a public relations game.'

'Public relations issues are inevitable when you're part of Kite Industries,' Pollack said. 'You must learn to live with that, to let people like me spin your story.'

'Even when I'm accused of murder?'

'As things stand, the police have no evidence on which to hold you. Is there anything you want to tell us today, in confidence? It will go no further than this room.'

'I watch TV,' Luke said. 'I thought lawyers weren't meant to ask questions they didn't already know the answers to.'

'That's true in court,' Pollack said, 'but my role here is damage limitation. I need to know what we're up against. Whatever you've done, Luke, the situation can be salvaged. But only if we know what the situation is.'

'I've done nothing,' Luke said, 'except try to look after my sister.' He turned to his uncle, who was frowning in furious concentration. 'The thing I'd like to know is, what has my uncle done?'

'Apart from keeping this company afloat?' Mike asked. He was about to say more, but then his mobile rang. 'Hold on,' he said, looking at the display. 'I have to answer this.'

He listened for a few seconds, then said 'OK.' He put the phone down and gave a thin smile. 'We've tracked her down,' he said. 'She used her email last night.'

'Where is she?' Pollack asked.

'Krakow, Poland.'

Twenty-Three

KRAKOW

Megan waited until Tomas was on a break, then bought him a coffee.

'You want to stay here?' Tomas asked. 'How long?'

'A few weeks. But I could do with some work.'

'*Do with?* I don't understand.'

'I don't have enough money to live on. I could waitress, or work in a shop like you.'

Megan could see the youth's mind working as he tried to word a reply. Why did this pretty girl from a rich country want to hang around for more than a holiday?

'The money here is not good,' was all he said.

'I don't need much.'

Tomas shrugged. 'Maybe I can help you find work.'

'And a cheap place to live.'

'Cheap? If it is cheap, is not nice.'

'I'm used to roughing it,' Megan fibbed.

'*Roughing it?*' Tomas said, looking at Megan's expensively manicured nails. 'I don't understand.'

'I'll stay anywhere,' Megan said.

'OK. I phone some friends. I'll come by your hotel after

work. Maybe we can go for a drink, yes?'

'Yes. That'd be nice.' She grinned. 'What time?'

'Seven?'

'Fine.'

'Maybe we go to a club. Prozak? You heard of it?'

'A club called Prozak? No.'

'Lot of English go there.'

'I don't want to see lots of English people,' Megan told him. 'Take me to a place where only Poles go.'

'OK.' Tomas gave her an open, naïve smile, and she fleetingly wondered whether he was *too* nice. It was hard to trust anyone these days. He put away his phone.

'Later.' Tomas went back to work and Megan set off into the market square mid-afternoon sun.

She strolled into the old cloth hall to get some shade and tried on pieces of amber jewellery. She wasn't sure if amber was a good look when you had reddish hair. Didn't matter. She wasn't going to spend Grace's money on anything but essentials.

Walking back to the hotel, she passed a travel agent. There was a special offer on flights to Japan, which made her think of the mysterious email she'd received the night before. She checked the battery of her mobile – Luke's mobile. It was fine. When would Ethan ring? It felt good, having two more people on her side. Tomas was cute. Megan was seventeen and had never had a serious boyfriend. But could you go out with someone if you couldn't fully speak their language? Maybe, if you were interested enough, you learned. But Polish did sound difficult, with all those glottal stops. And could she really go out with a guy who worked in a store? Should she even trust him? *Shut up!* she told herself. *What kind of snob are you?*

Her feet were getting tired. She checked her wallet. Not a lot of money. She'd better get some more out, so that she could buy Tomas a drink. And eat. Restaurant meals would soon suck up money. There were bound to be places where she could buy sandwiches to eat in the park. Or, if she got a place with a kitchen, she could cook for herself. Not that she knew how to cook.

The hotel at last. The woman at Reception smiled.

'Do you know if you stay tomorrow yet?'

'I'll let you know tonight,' Megan said, noticing that the internet computer in the lobby was free. She sat down and logged on to her email. Three pieces of spam and one from the email address in Japan. She clicked it open.

They've located you. Email is not safe. You need to be as far away as possible. Come to Tokyo if you can. Do not use this account again. Double delete this message, then leave at once.

Leave at once? That was pretty paranoid. Megan double deleted the message. She went up to her room. How could she leave when she was meant to be meeting Tomas here at seven? She couldn't let him down, not after he'd been so helpful. She collected her nearly dry underwear and stuffed it into her knapsack. She'd forgotten to buy new stuff but the bag was already too heavy.

Who had tracked her down? Megan had better leave. Maybe if she invented some family crisis, the hotel would refund what she'd paid for a second night. But it was already mid-afternoon. She'd have to pay something. At least they spoke good English here. They'd understand.

She got into the lift and went down to Reception. The woman from before was explaining to a bulky, overdressed man that she could not comply with his request. 'Nobody with that name is staying here.'

Megan had a sinking feeling. She saw the man get out a photograph.

'I know she's here. She may be using another name.'

The receptionist looked over the man's shoulder and Megan's heart stopped. She didn't have her baseball cap on yet. There was no mistaking her long, reddish-brown hair. The receptionist met her eyes and Megan frantically shook her head, stepping backwards, back into the lift.

'I don't think so,' the receptionist said.

'You don't mind if I wait?' the man asked. His accent was American. Her uncle had sent him after her.

She pressed 'down' and the lift took her to the basement, where there was a laundry room and a room with a table tennis table. Two girls were playing ping-pong. Both wore T-shirts and shorts. One was the American blonde who had spoken to Megan at breakfast. The other was a giant, over six feet tall.

'Is there a way out down here?' Megan asked.

'The exit is on the next floor,' said the blonde girl, helpfully rather than sarcastically.

'I know that. There's a guy waiting there who's been hitting on me. He's a real pain. I need to get past him.'

'Those Polish guys are mostly sweet. Just tell him straight out if you're not interested. He'll get the message.'

'This guy's American. He's a little creepy. I'm afraid of him. I think he followed me to the hotel.'

The girls stopped playing. 'Want us to distract him for you?' the taller one said.

'Would you? That'd be great.'

Megan described what he was wearing.

'Sounds overdressed. Has it cooled down out there yet?'

'It's just about bearable,' Megan said.

She followed the two girls up in the lift. It was risky, trusting strangers this way, but she had to get away quickly. She stuffed her hair into her baseball cap and put on her sunglasses.

'We'll take the stairs,' the tall girl said. 'He won't see us coming.'

'Thanks so much. You're stars,' Megan said. She hung back as the girls climbed the stairs. They turned into the lobby. Megan heard them swing into action.

'Are you the guy from the credit card company? I feel so stoopid, losing my Mastercard on my first day in Poland.'

Megan swept past them, depositing her keycard on the desk. She gave the receptionist a tight grin and was at the door before she allowed herself a glance back. The two American girls were still tightly in front of their co-patriot, who was seeking their help.

'I'm looking for this English girl. You may have seen her using the internet. Have you . . .'

Megan couldn't be sure, but she thought she recognized the guy. She had glimpsed him before. He was the man behind the wheel of the car that ran over Grace.

Out on the street, Megan walked as fast as she could.

Maybe she should take a cab straight to the airport. But that would be the first place the American would look if he worked out that she'd got away. Then she remembered the travel agent's. Would it still be open?

She remembered the way, two streets to her right, on Starowisina. A five-minute walk, less if she sprinted. Working up a sweat, she charged her way past cafés and restaurants to the main road, where the trams ran, overflowing with people heading home after the working day. Megan thought about what she would have to do. She couldn't go to Japan. It was thousands of miles away. The language was impossible.

The travel agent's with the cheap Japan offer was about to close. A guy only a little older than Tomas was locking the door.

'Excuse me,' Megan said. 'I need to get out of Krakow, tonight! Can you help me?'

The guy looked at his watch and shrugged. 'Sure.'

Inside the office, Megan took off her cap, shook her long hair out and gave the travel agent her cheesiest smile. She'd use whatever feminine wiles she had to get the best deal.

'English, huh? Where do you want to go?'

'Another hemisphere. Japan maybe. I see you have an offer.'

'You're coming back to Krakow?'

'Probably not.'

'The deal in the window is for return flights, booked well in advance. You said you want to travel tonight?'

'Sooner the better.'

'I might be able to get you a cheap stand-by. They sometimes dump tickets. Let me look at the computer.'

He took a couple of minutes. 'It's not good. There is a

flight tonight but I can't get any discounts on it. Wait, there is a way. How would you like to go to Sydney?'

Megan hadn't been to Australia since she was a kid. 'You can fly to Sydney from here?'

'No, but you can fly to Tokyo, stop over there and travel on to Sydney. I can do you a cheap deal on that trip. And if you don't use the flight to Sydney, you'll still be better off than if you take a one-way flight to Tokyo.'

'It's a deal. Let's do it.'

Megan booked an evening flight to Tokyo, where she was to have a two-day stopover. As soon as her credit card had gone into the computer, she began to worry. What if the guy at the hotel had found out that she was staying there under the name Grace Thompson? But it was too late to worry about that. What mattered now was whether Grace's credit card would go through. Megan tried not to look nervous as she waited for the machine to whirr its authorization. She could easily have gone over the card's credit limit.

'Want me to call you a taxi?' the young travel agent said. He wore a big smile, for he'd just made a good sale. Megan checked out how many zlotys she had left. Enough.

'OK, thanks.' The credit card machine began to print out the slip. Relieved, Megan got out her mobile.

'Tomas, I'm sorry. I have to leave Poland.'

'When?'

'Now. I can't explain, but thanks for your help. Be lucky.'

She hung up, hoping he wouldn't call back. He'd never know it, but this kiss-off phone call was probably the best luck she could have given him. Being around Megan was dangerous.

Twenty-Four

At a plush office in Whitehall, Ethan Thompson tried to explain what he wanted. His mother, the minister, wasn't having any of it.

'The girl's dead. She can't inherit. Why does it matter what her father's will said?'

'A will's a public document, isn't it?'

'Yes, but it doesn't become public until probate is complete, which can take months and months. Why do you need to know what's in it now?'

'The terms of the will may explain Megan's murder.'

Mum looked at him carefully. 'I didn't know you were so fond of her.'

'She was Grace's best friend. I've known her since she was twelve. I want to get to the bottom of what happened.'

'That's not a good enough reason for me to get involved, Eef. Ministers aren't meant to interfere in matters outside their jurisdiction. It could get me into trouble.'

'Even though the first attempt to murder her nearly killed your daughter?' Ethan insisted.

'That would give me an excuse, if it were true, but not a reason.'

Mum was tough. Ethan thought for a moment. He was

meant to keep a secret. Only he couldn't see a way around it.

'I promised not to tell but ... Megan isn't dead. I spoke to her this morning. She's in hiding, scared for her life. I promised to help her. And I know that you'll want to help her too.'

Luke was going crazy. Mike had told him to go home, said he'd tell him what was going on later. He'd spent the whole, boring day holed up in the Village, waiting to be arrested again. Nobody had called, not even his mom.

What was Megan doing in Krakow? Luke considered going to the police, telling them what he thought his uncle was up to. But he didn't know enough and might only incriminate himself. Then, finally, Mom came home. The fireworks started.

'What's going on?' Luke shouted at her. 'Why is Uncle Mike trying to track down Megan? Was it him who had Maria killed?'

Crystal got snippy. 'Calm down. Your uncle has you and your sister's best interests at heart. He wants to get to her before the terrorists do.'

'What terrorists? I don't believe there were any terrorists after her, or me. Admit it, Mom. Mike knew about the attack on Maria. He was behind it!'

'That's a terrible accusation.'

'Only if it isn't true.'

'Have a drink. If you can get over yourself for a minute I'll explain everything.'

Luke sank into the squashy, plush, Italian leather sofa Mom had just bought for the new apartment. His mother made herself a vodka and tonic, then began to talk.

'Mike's not a saint,' Crystal said. 'And you know I'm not. But we both have your best interests at heart, sweetie. We've always been there for you, both of us.'

'I know. So?'

'Your father's will came as a shock. That he would leave the whole business to Megan, with so little for you or Mike.'

'I wasn't expecting anything,' Luke asserted. All his life he had been the accidental son, the unwanted heir. He was grateful to Crystal, for choosing to have him, for bringing him up as best she could. But the gratitude he felt for his father's help was grudging. Their relationship was contaminated in every possible way. It would be better, he often thought, if he had never known Jack Kite, if he didn't bear his name.

'Mike wanted to help you. And me.'

And himself, Luke thought but didn't say.

'There was one thing we didn't count on,' Crystal said, 'which was that you and Megan would become close after Jack's death. That wasn't in the plan.'

'What plan?'

'Be quiet and listen for a minute. Sometimes it's best if you don't know everything. You have to trust your mother. I've never lied to you. But sometimes I've kept things back. Like the full provisions of the will. Like what happens to the money if Megan doesn't survive until her eighteenth birthday.'

'What happens?' Luke asked, his body tensing.

'You get it.'

KRAKOW

Megan had two hours to kill airside. She figured she was safe here. Airports had high security. Maybe she could figure out a way to spend the next five weeks in airports, only emerging when she reached her eighteenth. Tokyo airport was sure to be huge. No, Sydney would be a better place to hide in plain sight. There were bound to be lots of girls with freckles and long reddish-brown hair around.

She only had a few zlotys left, enough for a coffee, no more. But she had credit on her phone that would be of no use once she left Poland. She called Grace. It went straight to voicemail, so she called Ethan. He answered on the second ring.

'Megan. Still in Poland?'

'Yes, but this number won't work for much longer. I've got a ticket that takes me to Tokyo, then Sydney. How's Grace?'

'She's good. The operation was a success.'

'That's great. I tried to ring her earlier.'

'She was in some pain so they gave her a sleeping pill.'

'Did you get anywhere with what I asked about earlier?'

Megan heard Ethan take a deep breath.

'Yeah. Mum got Special Branch to look into it. She only just called. I'm still digesting what she said.'

'What did you find out?' Megan asked.

'That your family is arranging your funeral for next week.'

'What?'

'I don't know how they got round the business of the death certificate, but the body's going to be cremated. After

151

that happens, nobody will be able to prove if it was or wasn't you.'

'They must know I'm still alive. Who identified me?'

'Your uncle. He flew over earlier today.'

'Then that proves it's him – Uncle Mike's behind all this. Makes sense. He inherits everything, doesn't he?'

'It's not as simple as that,' Ethan said. 'What were you told about the will?'

'If I'm dead,' Megan said, trying to remember the short conversation where Luke reported what his mother had told him, 'then Uncle Mike inherits everything. Is that right?'

'The will's still in probate and there are complications. Mum got Special Branch to press your family's solicitor. He wouldn't give them much at first, said there were family privacy and company stock price considerations to consider. But they're good at bullying, these government agents.'

'Hurry up, Eef!' Megan insisted. 'My credit will run out any minute. Does my uncle inherit anything or doesn't he?'

'In the short term, he's in charge, as he would have been anyway, until your eighteenth. Since you're meant to have died before you could inherit, forty percent of the Kite Industries shares that would have gone to you go to Mike.'

'Only forty percent?'

'The rest – a controlling interest – are held in trust.'

'Who by? When until?'

'Your uncle will be in control for another two years, until your brother turns eighteen. Then he becomes the majority shareholder. Your brother Luke will own Kite Industries.'

Megan was staggered. She didn't always like Luke. He could be grumpy and childish and resentful. But he was her brother and she loved him. And she thought she knew when he was lying.

'You think Luke's part of this?'

'He has to be.'

Twenty-Five

TOKYO

The bus from Narita airport took an hour. The train was cheaper but the underground looked difficult to navigate if you had no Japanese. They passed rice fields and endless suburbs. Megan tried the mobile with the Polish SIM. Useless.

A cityscape appeared, a riot of tall, colourful, modern buildings. As they got to its centre, the bus crossed a wide river. This was Tokyo's only similarity to Krakow. Poland was visiting the past. Tokyo was the future. Megan got out of the bus at Tokyo station and began to walk.

She'd picked up a free map at Narita but soon realized she would have been better off buying a compass. Then at least she'd know which direction she was walking in. Few signs were in English, while the Japanese language was hieroglyphics to her. The map had the English names for subway stations. Even so, Megan found the layout impossible to follow. Maybe the Japanese felt the same way about the London underground.

It was early evening but the streets were still swelteringly hot and crowded. Megan needed a place to stay and she needed cash. Tokyo was said to be one of the most expensive cities in the world. Uncle Mike used to tell stories about the city when he ran the Kite Industries office here. She caught a street name in English, a name he'd mentioned. Ginza. Where all the top stores were. From the signs outside, it looked like many of the stylish, high buildings had different stores on every floor.

There were restaurants everywhere. The prices didn't look too bad. There were photos of dishes that you could point at. Only she wasn't hungry yet. There had been a light supper and breakfast on the plane.

Where was the hotel district? Megan tried asking passers-by. It soon became clear that the average Japanese person knew little more English than the average English person knew Japanese. She went up some side streets. The first hotel she tried to go into appeared to be plush, but turned out to be a bank. Then she found the Tōbu hotel, which looked promising. The guy behind the desk spoke good English. 'A single room for two nights. No problem.' He quoted a price that, even in London, would have been dear. 'If I could just get your credit card . . .'

Megan handed the card over and, dry-mouthed, took a complimentary mint from the bowl on the counter. She looked at the brochure which mentioned the hotel's business centre. Megan might use the internet there to contact her mystery 'friend' in Japan. This time, she would not make the mistake of using her own email account. She'd set up a new one.

'I'm sorry, Miss, there's a problem with this card. Do you have another one?'

'Eh, no.' Megan had Grace's cash card but didn't know how much there was in that account. Probably not enough for a swish hotel. 'Could you try it again, please?'

'Of course.'

Megan thought quickly. She'd asked Ethan to see if the credit limit on Grace's card could be increased. It was probably naive to think he would have got it done overnight. Either she had maxed the card out or the credit card company had stopped her credit because she was using it abroad without warning.

'Still not working, I'm sorry.'

'OK,' Megan said. 'Can you tell me where to find a cash machine around here?'

It took a while to explain what a cash machine was, then a few more minutes to work out that Tokyo had relatively few ATMs.

'If you are short of money,' the concierge said, 'you could try one of the capsule hotels. Very basic, but very cheap.'

'Good idea,' Megan said. Mike had told her about those, too: hotels with rooms little bigger than coffins. Businessmen used them when they missed the last train home. No showers, room service or place to leave lots of luggage. But anonymous. Cheap and anonymous was what she needed at the moment.

After several wrong turns, she found a cash machine. It let her withdraw a hundred pounds' worth of yen, but gave no indication of how much money was left in Grace's account. At least Megan could eat and pay for a room for the night.

8.30 p.m. Megan found a noodle place that was still full of office workers. She ordered a bowl of something by pointing at a young woman's meal. It came quickly, teppan noodles in a hot broth with a few pieces of pork floating around. Only when she'd gobbled it down did she realize how hungry she'd been.

The place was closing. She paid quickly and returned to Ginza. It began to rain, hard. She looked up. As the city grew dark, the city became endless splashes of technicolour. Ginza was like New York's Fifth Avenue, advanced about a century. Like Fifth Avenue, she saw, it had an Apple store, this one going up several floors. She wondered if it had free email.

The rain began to pour, so she went inside. She'd find the capsule hotel later. The Apple store was open for another hour, but she couldn't tell if it had free internet. The first floor was all iPods and iPhones. She went up in the lift. On the second, there were accessories and some computers, but they weren't net connected. She stepped out on to the third floor to find a large lecture theatre. The lecturer was pointing at a screen. A dozen geeks gazed at what appeared to be a preview for a new operating system. Megan got back into the lift. One floor left.

At the back of this floor, looking over Ginza, were banks of computers, each with an open web browser. Several were unoccupied. She took one in the farthest corner and quickly set up a free email account. She chose the username *redkite*. Then she emailed her mystery friend. *I'm in Tokyo. Where are you? Can you help me?*

After that, she browsed websites for a few minutes, trying to see if there was any news about her, her dad, or Kite Industries. The share price was still way down, she saw. The

Kite Industries stock she was due to inherit had lost nearly a third of its value since Dad's death. Before going, she checked the new email account, but there was no reply. She left the store, heading back to Tokyo station and the capsule hotel.

It wasn't hard to find. Inside, by the reception desk, there was even a sign in English. It read *Men Only*. Megan cursed. She was about to return to the street when the woman behind the counter called to her. She spoke in Japanese but Megan understood her gesticulations. There was another capsule hotel a short distance away. This one did take women.

The second hotel was a little harder to find, tucked down a narrow alley. There was a queue of sheepish, bespectacled Japanese men. It took Megan ten minutes to get to the desk. Here, a brusque young man pointed at a sign. *No English*. He seemed to be saying that the hotel was for Japanese people only, but Megan wasn't having it.

'You're not allowed to say that!' she insisted. 'That's racist. You must have laws against it. I want a room!' She got out a pile of yen. The man shrugged, took some of her money, then gave her a plastic key card with a number on it and another key which she didn't understand the point of. Finally he handed her a thin towel and a single piece of soap.

Megan found the rooms easily enough. Everyone was going in that direction. Her pod was one of the lower ones, so somebody would be sleeping directly above her. One glance told her that the pod was too small to get undressed in, never mind stand up. The only place to wash and change appeared to be communal. There was no way that Megan was going to get undressed in front of a bunch of drunken Japanese men – whether or not they had their glasses on.

Someone tugged her T-shirt at the shoulder. Megan bristled, but when she turned, it was a slender young woman her own age. The Japanese woman pointed to the far end of the dormitory, where there was a room with a female silhouette on the door. Megan bowed in thanks, hoping that this was the right etiquette. On the way to the bathroom, she found the small lockers where you could leave your possessions overnight. That was what the second key was for. She put her knapsack in it, then washed and changed for bed. Only one other woman came in while she was using the bathroom.

When Megan returned to her pod, the air was already thick with snores. She crawled in and turned on the TV. There were no English language channels. She watched game shows for half an hour, then stuffed tissues in her ears and tried to sleep.

The first alarms went off at five. At six, Megan gave up hope of trying to get any more kip, and got up. One thing she hadn't noticed the night before: there was a café and a shop with racks that were filled, not only with snacks, but with cheap underwear and business shirts. She bought herself a white shirt and three spare pairs of knickers, then set out to face the day.

Twenty-Six

BROOKLYN

'You inherit everything?' Andy asked.

'A majority holding. Even with the fall in the stock price the shares are worth billions and billions of dollars.'

'That's outstanding!'

'I guess.' Luke could hardly tell his friend that Megan was still alive, but in great danger. He'd had to tell someone what Mike had told him. It was too mega to keep to himself.

'I mean, I know you'd rather your sister was alive but it was kind of unfair, her getting the whole company, wasn't it?'

'I guess my dad had his reasons.'

'Everybody has their reasons. Doesn't make them right.'

'Whatever.' Luke didn't want to discuss this further. He didn't want the money and he wasn't going to get the money. 'Let's play *Guitar Hero*, we haven't been on that for days.'

Andy's tastes were more heavy metal than Luke's but, this afternoon, Luke was happy to indulge his friend, to throw himself into jamming along with rhythmic, crunchy noise. It stopped him from thinking about Uncle Mike for a few seconds.

Uncle Mike wasn't like his father. When you got through

to Dad, he always gave a straight answer, even if it wasn't the one you wanted to hear. Mike avoided answering, or changed the question around so that you didn't find out what you wanted to find out and felt bad about asking in the first place. The day before, when Luke had questioned him about Maria's murder, Mike's reply was terse.

'The situation's complicated. There are some things you're better off not knowing.'

'How come?'

'The police have already questioned you about that girl's unfortunate death. They might come for you again. You're not responsible. You don't need to know the full details. End of.'

'What about Megan? Is she still in Krakow?'

'I don't know. We're trying to track her down, get her safe. I'm praying she hasn't fallen into the hands of the people who killed your father.'

'And who are those people, precisely?'

'If we knew who the ACW were, they'd be in custody. Luke, you need to keep a low profile. It might be best if you returned to your friend in Brooklyn. Leave all this to me.'

Despite deep misgivings, Luke had done as Mike suggested. He felt safer here, in a Brooklyn brownstone, than he did in the Village. He was conflicted about Megan. It was no surprise Dad put her ahead of him in the will. Dad knew how Luke felt about his money. If he hadn't been such a workaholic, making his fortune, Jack Kite might have been a better father. If Luke somehow were to inherit, he would, he decided, give everything away. That'd really screw up Uncle Mike.

'That is totally the wrong chord!'

'Sorry, my mind's somewhere else.'

'Want to talk about it?'

TOKYO

On Ginza, the Apple store wasn't open yet. While she waited, Megan found a food store. She bought a carton of orange juice and some sweet cakes. This felt so weird. She was in Japan at seven in the morning. It was already hot and humid. She knew nobody and had nothing to do except survive. In an odd way, she had never been so free, so anonymous.

A queue of people, mostly travellers like herself, charged to the fourth-floor computers when the store opened. The email was waiting for her when she logged on.

Meet me at Shibuya Station tonight. Wait by the dog statue at seven. I will find you. And don't worry. All will be fine.

Megan had seen the movie *Lost in Translation*. She remembered that Shibuya was Tokyo's equivalent of Soho, tacky and trendy in equal measures. She would work out how to get there later. Megan surfed the net for a long while. Being on the net made her feel at home. Or, at least, in familiar surroundings. She didn't have a home, as such, hadn't for years. School had been the most constant presence in her life.

The computers were starting to clear. Somebody had left a copy of *The Rough Guide to Tokyo* in English at one of the other terminals. Megan had spotted it five minutes ago. She waited a couple of minutes to see if they came back for it. She'd never stolen anything before, but needs must.

Back on the street, Megan consulted the book on how the metro system worked. Once you got over the Japanese language it was pretty much like the London underground, only not so expensive. Also, there seemed to be two different systems in place. You had to get different tickets for one kind or the other. She had hours and hours before she was due to meet her 'friend'. Might as well keep on the move, be a tourist. She found the nearest station, descended the stairs, located a ticket machine and bought a book of tickets. She was good to go.

Megan took the Ginza line to the last stop, Asakusa, which had the city's most famous Buddhist temple. The train was fast, quiet. The only other Westerner was a man in a safari suit at the other end of the carriage. Even down here, many of the Japanese wore white face masks. Megan had seen a lot of these above ground. She assumed they were to protect against air pollution, but maybe they were more worried about catching germs from their fellow commuters.

Out of the station, she passed through an enormous red gate, beneath a massive paper lantern, into Nakamise-dōri, the famous shopping street that ran from Kaminarimon Gate to Hozomon Gate. Crowds pushed through endless rows of covered stalls. Megan tried not to be distracted by the fancy kimonos, elaborate stationery, incense, statues, fans and other trinkets on sale. She loved to window shop, but it was no fun when you were on the run and had nothing to spend.

Before she got to the temple itself, Megan noticed a large, bronze, covered bowl which sent out white plumes of smoke. People wafted the pungent smoke on to their backs. According to the guidebook, the smoke represented the breath of the gods and had healing powers. Megan wasn't superstitious, but turned away from the temple, allowing the smoke to drift on to her back. That was when she spotted the man from the underground, following her.

The man in the safari suit was white and averted his eyes as soon as Megan's met his, pretending to take a photograph of the incense bowl. Megan stepped quickly into the crowd. She didn't want to be photographed with her baseball cap, shorts, T-shirt and knapsack. With a current photo, Uncle Mike – or whoever – would be easily able to track her down. She followed the crowd into the huge, beautiful temple. People bought charms and rolled-up papers, which seemed to promise good luck. They threw coins into a huge wooden coffer. The man tailing Megan was just outside the temple, in his light coloured safari suit and aviator sunglasses. The sun reflected on his balding head. He didn't seem to have spotted Megan yet. Was she being paranoid? Could he have followed her from the Apple store? Or was he simply another tourist, like herself, visiting one of the most popular and historic spots in the city?

Loud drums began to sound. According to the guidebook, this meant it was ten o'clock. Tourists hurried into the temple to take in the priests as they chanted sutras beneath the gilded canopy of the temple's altar. Megan used this chance to move swiftly in the opposite direction, pushing her way through the human tide until she was back amongst the busy stalls.

At the station, she bought one of the white face masks that so many of the Japanese wore. With her hair pushed back, sunglasses and a change of T-shirt, she would be very hard to spot. She got on the first train out, confident that she hadn't been followed. Megan still had nine hours to kill before she met her mystery 'friend'.

BROOKLYN

Andy brought up the *Wall Street Journal* website. He opened all the stories about Kite Industries with multiple tabs, then flicked between them. Andy's dad was a broker. When he and Luke were kids, they both wanted to be comic book artists. These days Andy planned to major in Economics and work in movie accounting. He got up to speed quickly.

'Am I going broke?' Luke asked.

'Hardly. Kite have got all these valuable patents and a really good income stream. The current stock price isn't about value. It's about speculation. Software and internet stocks are almost always overpriced because they're in a sexy area. But death's not sexy. Also, Kite Industries was perceived as being largely about your dad. Once he died, confidence crashed. So the stocks lost half their value. But they've started climbing again, because speculators see a profitable company with shares going cheap. If Kite Industries continues to be successful, the shares could easily be worth a whole lot more by the time you inherit.'

'Maybe you can be my finance manager,' Luke said.

'I expect they have people at Kite who can handle that,' Andy told him. 'I won't be qualified for seven years, minimum.'

'If I inherit, there'll always be a job for you, bro',' Luke said, then remembered he'd decided to give the company away.

'Appreciated,' Andy said, and began flicking between the tabs again. 'Kite stock took a big hit, bigger than the commentators were expecting. They're saying Megan's murder and the terrorist thing panicked stockholders and the shares are still seriously undervalued.'

'I thought Uncle Mike managed to steady the ship.'

'Somebody bought a lot of shares when the price hit rock bottom. That helped arrest the fall. They climbed a bit and have held steady for a couple of days.'

'So Mike's succeeding.'

'The price is still volatile. And look at these articles: your uncle's been taking a lot of criticism for not speaking to the press. "*It's hardly the behaviour of somebody intent on saving the company*," this reporter says. Sounds a little fishy.'

'Fishy or not, I've got no power to affect things for another two years. What do you think I should do?'

Andy thought for a minute.

'If it was me, I'd ask for a big allowance, take it easy, only study stuff that you find interesting or that'll help you run one of the world's biggest companies. But, most of all, chill.'

'Easier said than done,' Luke said. 'Thing is, there's something I haven't told you.'

'What?'

'This is just between us, OK? You'll understand why when I tell you.'

'OK. What is it?'

'Megan, my sister, she's still alive. In fact, you've met her. I told you her name was Ginger.'

'You're kidding!'

Luke explained some of what had happened.

'I still don't understand. Why is she pretending to be dead?'

'She isn't pretending, not exactly. The police announced that she was murdered in London but that was somebody else. I'm pretty sure both the girl who died in London and Maria were killed by the same people who are trying to kill Megan.'

'Terrorists?' Andy asked. 'This so-called ACW?'

'I don't think so,' Luke replied. 'I figure the person behind it is much closer to home.'

Twenty-Seven

TOKYO

Rush hour slowed Megan down. She was getting used to the way Japanese underground stations had multiple exits. Some went straight into stores or malls. Others led on to the street. But Shibuya was the most confusing of all. She came up an escalator and there was a huge window to her right. Beneath was a little plaza, at the centre of which was the statue of the dog that she was aiming for. And she was already late.

Megan went one way, found herself in one DVD store, then another. None of the exits she tried took her outside. She kept finding herself in different parts of the shopping centre. She doubled back on herself, but this didn't work. She got to a booking hall for the station, then the platform she'd first come in on. Finally, after ten or fifteen minutes, she was in a boutique, hyperventilating.

Megan looked at her watch. Nearly twenty past seven. This was disastrous. The only good thing to come out of her being late was that she could be pretty sure nobody was following her. She returned to the walkway with the big window. Young Japanese people surrounded the dog, many drinking and smoking, some obviously alone, waiting on dates. Impossible to tell if her date was already there, getting frustrated with her. There seemed to be a steady stream of people coming out into the plaza. Where were they coming from? Could that be it? Megan doubled back on herself again. This time she took an inconspicuous exit which she'd assumed led to a store. It didn't. A minute later, she was on the ground level, heading for the statue of the dog.

She'd read the story of Hachikō in the *Rough Guide*. Last century, the Akita dog faithfully followed his master, a university professor, to the station every morning, then returned in the evening to greet him. One day, his master died while at work. Hachikō continued to come in the evenings. The dog arrived at the same time every day for ten years, until its death. Local people were so impressed that, the year before Hachikō died, they put up a bronze statue of the Akita dog. The statue soon became a famous meeting place.

'Miss Kite?' A slender Japanese man, two inches smaller than her, stepped out from the crowd. 'My name is Toru.'

'I'm pleased to meet you,' Megan said, shaking his hand.

'We must get out of here quickly. People are looking for you.'

'I know but before we do . . . who are you? We've never met before. All I know is that you sent me some cryptic emails.'

'You're right to be cautious. I will tell you all when we get to a place that is more private. Until then, it is enough that you know one thing.' He paused, then leaned up and whispered in her ear. 'Your father sent me.'

LONDON

At last, Grace had been allowed to come home. Now the arguments started in earnest.

'You've got to check that the body they're burying really is Megan!' Grace insisted to her mum over a late breakfast.

'We don't have any right to look at a corpse,' Mum replied.

'If you don't, then who does? Once the body's been cremated, that's it. She'll be officially dead. Her uncle and her brother will inherit everything. But Megan's still alive! People are after her.'

Mum was having none of it. 'I'm sorry, Grace. I know you've been through a traumatic time. Losing Megan must have made everything worse. But these conversations you think you had with Megan make no sense. Either it was somebody playing a prank or you were hallucinating because of the anaesthetic. That's quite common when you spend a lot of time in bed. It gets hard to distinguish between dreams and what really happened.'

Ethan watched his sister's face flare, her cheeks almost the same colour as her auburn hair.

'I don't *believe* this! Ethan, tell her.'

'I spoke to Megan, too, Mum.'

'You spoke to someone who you thought was Megan. But you hardly know the girl. I've read how obsessed teenage girls get with death, with ghosts talking from the afterlife, all that cheap quasi-religion, superstitious rubbish. I'm surprised at you falling for it, Ethan. This is dangerous talk. Mike Kite is an important person, a respected businessman

170

who oozes integrity. To suggest that he's trying to kill his own niece, it's preposterous.'

Grace got involved again. 'You admitted the police have no evidence of this environmental terrorist group that's after her.'

'No evidence is not the same as it not being true.' Mum looked out of the window. Her car had arrived. 'It's time for me to go to the Home Office. I'm sorry, both of you, but I think you're deluded. Megan's funeral is in six days. You might want to buy some dark, sombre clothes to wear at it.'

'I'm stony broke,' Ethan pointed out. 'I maxed out my card in Africa.'

'More fool you. Use Grace's card to get a suit.'

'I can't use her money.'

'It's family money. Your father pays it off every month.'

As Mum left, Ethan and Grace exchanged worried glances.

'You should have told her about the credit card,' Ethan said. 'It would prove that Megan's alive.'

'Or that somebody stole the card. If I told them about it, they'd cancel it.'

'I forgot to tell you,' Ethan said. 'You had a call from the card company. I think Megan maxed it out already. I asked, but they wouldn't raise the credit limit without Dad's say-so.'

Grace checked her bank balance online. 'I still have over a hundred quid on my cash card account. Megan can access that. She took out a hundred pounds yesterday.'

'It's not a lot though, is it?' Ethan thought for a moment. 'Does it say where she took the money out?'

'A bank in Ginza? Know where that is?'

'Tokyo.'

'At least we know she's alive.'

'You're sure? You're sure it's really her we've been talking to and not some creepy school-friend playing games, like Mum suggested?'

'Of course I'm sure,' Grace replied. 'The question is, how do we stop the funeral?'

BROOKLYN

The phone call from his mother was brief and to the point.

'Your sister's funeral is next Thursday. Your uncle's booking tickets for us to fly on Wednesday. If you want me to help you find a dark suit, it'll need to be before then.'

'Megan isn't dead,' Luke informed her, tersely. 'I'm not going to a fake funeral.'

'I know you've got this into your head, Luke, but it's not true.'

'What is this?' Luke asked. 'You were there last week when I saw the bike outside the condo. You and Mike weren't arguing then when I told you that she was alive. Me and Mike went looking for her.'

Mom put on her rare don't-mess-with-me voice. 'That was then and this is now, Luke. Megan's dead and I don't want you sharing those doubts with anybody. Your uncle's gone to considerable trouble to make sure this goes smoothly. If you screw it up, you'll be the one to suffer most. Give me a call when you want to buy a suit.' She hung up on him.

Luke recounted the phone call to Andy. 'My mom's

completely in Uncle Mike's pocket,' he told him. 'But I won't let Mike pull my strings, too. I need to go to the office, now, get him to level with me.'

'You can't confront your uncle,' Andy argued. 'It's clear he's on the level. If you're right, he could have killed you already, then everything would come to him.'

'He still could mean to kill me. Maybe I should go on the run, like Megan.'

'Or maybe you should go over to the dark side, embrace it, like your uncle seems to have done.'

'You're saying I should sit back while my uncle hunts down Megan, has her killed?'

'Your sister's already dead.'

'But you met her!'

'You never said she was your sister when she was here. I met someone called Ginger, who you say is travelling under the name of Grace. But your half-sister's gone. They're cremating her next week. A multi-billion-dollar corporation is about to fall into your lap. Embrace it, Luke!'

'Since when did you join the Young Republicans?'

'Since when did you want to be poor?'

'And what if Mike decides to murder me, too, once I've inherited?' Luke asked.

'You can always leave everything to me, dude. That'd screw him up.'

Things were getting surreal, Luke decided. Andy wasn't being Andy, not the Andy he used to know. Luke didn't know how seriously to take him. Money changed people, Dad used to say. Crystal was being much nicer since they moved into the Greenwich Village condo.

Andy had a point. According to the rest of the world, Megan was dead. The only people who thought otherwise were Luke, Mike and his mother. Life would be simpler if Megan really were gone, if the girl he'd just spent a few days with turned out not to have been the real Megan.

The doorbell rang and Andy went to get it. 'For you!' he yelled.

Luke joined his friend in the hallway. It was the Brooklyn police department, the two officers who'd kept him in overnight when they interrogated him about Maria's murder.

'We have some questions for you concerning the death of your sister,' the one in the leather jacket said.

'Go ahead,' Luke told them.

'Not here,' the suit said. 'We'd like you to accompany us to the station.'

TOKYO

Toru linked his arm through Megan's and took her across the biggest junction she had ever crossed, bigger than Trafalgar Square. While the pedestrian lights were on, streams of people crossed in multiple directions. Everyone seemed to know where they were going, but Megan couldn't get her head around it at all. She was totally discombobulated by the news that Dad was alive. She wanted to believe it but daren't let herself.

'You're sure you weren't followed?' Toru asked Megan.

'I got so lost in the mall, I'd have noticed,' Megan said. 'I thought a man was following me earlier, but it may have been a coincidence. I managed to lose him all the same.'

'Good, good,' Toru said, pointing the way up a narrow street that was full of bars, restaurants and electronics stores. They walked uphill until the early evening crowds began to thin.

'We can talk here,' Toru said, guiding her into a dark, badly lit space that looked like a strip club. Behind the red curtains was a quiet bar with small tables, serving soft drinks, saki and beer. Tired and apprehensive, Megan took off her face mask and ordered coffee. Toru took green tea.

'Thank you for coming to Japan,' he said. 'It can't have been easy.'

'Thank you for warning me to get out of Krakow,' she said. 'I got your email just in time. How did you know they would come for me so quickly?'

'When I told your father that you had replied to my email, he told me that it would be monitored, that your uncle would send somebody at once. So I sent the warning.'

'Why you? Why couldn't my father write himself?'

'Your father is not a well man.'

'But he was saved from the helicopter crash?'

'Yes. I'm afraid I do not know all the details. I have spoken with Mr Kite only by telephone.'

Again, Megan tried not to get her hopes up. And she was hearing cracks in the story.

'So you've never met my father?'

'Not in person, no.'

'Why is he pretending to be dead?'

'To prevent further attempts on his life. He did not anticipate that you would be in such danger and apologizes for your situation. He has been recovering from his injuries.'

'Where? Can you take me there?'

'Possibly. In time, when I am sure it is safe.' Toru looked at his watch.

'Are we waiting for someone?'

'You were late. I want us to keep on the move. You have all your possessions with you?'

'What little there is, yes.'

More people arrived in the bar but Megan didn't look up. She had something urgent on her mind.

'Tell me, who is responsible for the attacks on my father and me? Is it my uncle? Is my brother involved?'

Toru, she realized, was looking over her shoulder. Megan turned round. The man in the safari suit stood over her, a discomforting bulge beneath his right shoulder. He had taken off his sunglasses and his eyes were cold and grey. They were a killer's eyes. His accent was American.

'You're coming with me,' he said.

Twenty-Eight

BROOKLYN

The suit and the leather jacket escorted Luke to the station but the man asking the questions was British. He had a neutral accent. Upper class maybe. Luke wasn't good on British accents.

'You have dual nationality, I believe.' The interrogator was forty or so, greying at the temples but with smooth, lightly tanned skin. Not Luke's idea of a British copper.

Luke nodded. 'You'll have to tell me who you are and who you represent before I answer any questions.'

'Ian Trevelyan, Special Branch, representing her Majesty's Government,' the cop replied, then went straight on. 'You flew out of the UK eight days ago, the same day that your sister was murdered. Do I have that right?'

'As it turned out.' Luke's brain worked frantically. Was this the time to tell the truth about Megan being alive? Or should he follow Andy's advice and act as though Megan really was dead? He didn't know what Uncle Mike would advise. He did know that the choice was about to become stark. He was either on his uncle's side or he was on his own.

'According to our records, you didn't make it to Heathrow

until more than two hours after she was shot.'

'I don't know what time she was . . . are you suggesting that I had anything to do with her shooting? That's ridiculous!'

'It was ridiculous until we discovered that your father's will says that, in the event of your sister's death, you inherit the majority of Kite Industries shares.'

'I didn't know that.'

'Really? Your mother was at the will reading, I believe.'

'She didn't tell me.' This was true, he reminded himself. She didn't tell him at first.

'I find that very odd,' Trevelyan murmured. 'Can you tell me where you were at the time of your sister's death?'

'With my mom, getting ready to return to New York.'

'I see. The whole time?'

'I don't remember. I'd have to think.'

'I'd do that if I were you. We'll be questioning your mother. I'd like you to give me her new address.'

'Sure.' Luke wrote it down.

'Perhaps you could tell me about the explosion at your apartment building. That was quite a coincidence, wasn't it, happening the same day as your father's death?'

'Megan had a close call too,' Luke pointed out. 'I couldn't have had anything to do with it. I was in Brooklyn at the time.'

Trevelyan nodded. 'Nobody's suggesting that you acted alone, Luke. We are suggesting that you were involved. You were seen hurrying away from your home five minutes before the explosion.'

'It was a gas leak, not a bomb!'

'Actually, that's speculation. Investigators were unable to

prove the cause of the explosion one way or another.'

'News to me,' Luke said. 'I'm surprised that the ACW didn't claim responsibility, like they did for Dad's death.'

The Englishman exchanged amused glances with the American cops. 'Do you know what ACW stands for?'

'Against—'

'Hardly,' the suit interrupted. 'It stands for Association of Christian Writers.'

'Surely it means something different in Europe?'

'You're right,' Trevelyan said. 'In the UK, it stands for Arts Council Wales. You know, terrorists tend to be publicity conscious, so they don't use acronyms that are associated with other bodies. And they tend to go for something memorable. If they're real, that is. We have no evidence of any terrorist involvement in your father's death or that of your sister.'

'I see,' Luke mumbled.

'I intend to apply for an extradition order, to bring you to the UK for questioning.'

'But I haven't done anything!' Luke protested.

'Possibly so. But I should point out that coming with me voluntarily might well be in your best interests. The UK treats criminals under the age of eighteen much more leniently than the US does. Here, you could be tried as an adult.'

'What for?'

Trevelyan glanced at the cheap suit, who spoke.

'Accessory to murder.'

Luke shook his head. He needed his uncle's help, he realized. 'I want my lawyer,' he said. 'Get me Marcus Pollack.'

TOKYO

Before the balding man could reach for his gun, Megan kicked the table over. That drew the attention of everybody in the small bar. She yelled at the top of her voice. 'Yazuka! Gun!'

Pandemonium. Everybody got to their feet. They knew what the Yazuka was, and they knew what 'gun' meant, even if the white guy reaching for one didn't look much like a Japanese gangster. As everybody else stood, Megan ducked. She pushed her way in between the people piling through the door and squeezed her way out.

In the hot evening air, she ran downhill, heart pumping like crazy, along the narrow street, to the world's biggest pedestrian crossing. Rapid footsteps followed her.

She was in luck. The lights were changing. Megan forced her way in to the throng of people, getting ugly or bemused looks from pedestrians. She glanced behind her. No sign of her pursuer. Megan ducked her head and slowed down, reaching into her shorts pocket for her face mask. She put it on.

Too risky to go to the station, she decided. The American in the safari suit was bound to pursue her there. Head bowed, she moved with the crowd, on to a road dominated by electronics shops, passing vending machines that sold tiny toys in clear plastic capsules. When the crowd began to thin, she stepped into one of the busier stores, which sold comic books. She wished she were back in Brooklyn, with her brother and his friend Andy. He had been about to show her his comics, she remembered, when she saw the message, telling Luke to run.

Who had sent Luke that message? Maybe it wasn't Mike. Maybe that was Toru. But why? Megan would ask her Japanese friend if she were able to find him. She couldn't risk going to the Apple store again. The American must have followed her from there before. So she had to find another place with free email. A cheap hotel, maybe.

Suppose the balding American had captured Toru? That was unlikely. She'd heard the assassin coming after her. Megan had to find Toru. She had to connect with her father. But Toru hadn't actually met her father, she reminded herself. He could be working for somebody else who was spinning him a line.

Dad's being alive was too much to take in. She mustn't let it freak her out. If she was careless, Dad would survive, but she wouldn't. The first thing she had to do was find somewhere safe to stay tonight. She looked at her pocket map. Shibuya Station was too risky, but there was another station on the Ginza line nearby, Shinsen. She would go there.

LONDON

Grace was online, looking at her bank statements.

'You should go to Tokyo,' she told Ethan. 'Find her.'

'Do you know how big Tokyo is, how densely populated?'

'Yes, but not with white girls who have reddish-brown hair.'

'It's not going to happen, Grace. Not unless she gets in touch, tells us where to find her.'

'You always had a soft spot for her, didn't you?'

'Did not.'

'I've seen you checking her out.'

'I hardly know her,' Ethan insisted. Which was true. It was also true that he'd fancied Megan since she was fourteen, and they'd once got carried away at a party. But there was no way he'd ask out his sister's best friend. He noticed Grace's face light up. 'What is it?'

'She's just used the credit card again.'

'But she's over the limit!'

'When it's a small transaction the store doesn't check. It would take too long. This is just a few quid. Shibuya, Tokyo. So now we know where she is.'

'I've been to Tokyo,' Ethan said. 'Shibuya's bigger than the West End. Have you tried emailing again?'

'Not today. She's not replied to the other two I sent.'

'Probably wise. You can track any email down to a single computer. Even checking your account can be enough to trigger an alarm message if someone's determined to track you down. But if she bought a plane ticket to Tokyo, she'll have done it under your name. We need to find what airline she travelled on, then get in touch with them, say we've lost the ticket details.'

'We know she flew from Krakow to Tokyo.'

'That was two days ago. She may be on her way to Sydney by now.'

'And why Sydney?'

'She mentioned Sydney on the phone.'

'It doesn't make sense,' Grace said. 'She's never been to Japan before, or Australia as far as I'm aware. She can't know anybody there.'

'Maybe she wants to be as far away as possible.'

'You mean she doesn't want us to find her? I don't believe that,' Grace said. 'But I can't go after her, not in this state.'

'You have to be at the funeral,' Ethan said.

'I do, but you don't. You hardly knew her, remember?'

Ethan sighed. 'Let's not get ahead of ourselves. Do a websearch. Which airlines fly from Krakow to Tokyo?'

Twenty-Nine

TOKYO

They knew she was in Japan. It was time to leave. Megan had a plane ticket that would take her to Sydney this evening. She could head for the airport now, hide there. Or was that the first place her pursuers would look?

Using the computer in the hotel foyer, Megan checked the flight times. Then she checked the email account she had set up the day before. There was a message from Toru.

Did you get away? If you are safe, please reply and meet me on observation desk of the Mori tower in Roppongi Hills, 1pm. Very safe place with many tourists, you won't stand out. I will take you to your father.

Megan typed *I'll be there*. Then she buried her head in her hands. She couldn't believe she was going to be with Dad. And somewhere safe, a refuge. Megan pictured Dad in a temple in the country, surrounded by ninja warriors, being healed by a robed old man with a long, grey beard while beautiful women in kimonos served him tea. That would be Dad's idea of heaven.

Megan meant to leave as soon as she'd dried her hair, but she had to give it five more minutes. Whoever was tracing her email already knew she was in Tokyo. She might as well check her home email, see if Grace, Ethan or Luke had been in touch.

There was no message from Luke or Ethan, but there were three from Grace, the latest sent just this morning. Megan read all three and replied to the last. Grace was obviously aware that the email might be being accessed by Megan's enemies. She hadn't let on that Megan was using her identity, only mentioned that *I've put more money (£500) into your account but the credit card is at its limit, which cannot be increased. You should be able to get away with using it for small transactions, which retailers don't call in.* Megan had already worked this out, when she visited a chemist's near her cheap hotel. She deleted the whole exchange, then went back to her room and used the hairdryer.

Once outside the hotel, she threw her knapsack over her shoulder and put on her face mask. She put on her baseball cap and sunglasses, but did not tuck her hair beneath her shirt, which she'd bought at the capsule hotel yesterday. Her hair was now jet black. You would have to get near Megan before you realized that she was anything other than an unusually tall Japanese girl.

BROOKLYN

'This is preposterous,' Marcus Pollack told Trevelyan. 'It's ten at night. My client has been in custody for more than twenty-four hours. You don't have enough evidence for an extradition order.'

'We have two dead girls. Your client knew both of them and admits to being in the vicinity of both when they died. He doesn't have an alibi for either murder.'

'The same could be said for thousands of people.'

Luke was tired. He asked to speak to his lawyer alone.

'I'll have you out of here soon,' Pollack said, once the three police officers had left the room. 'They have nothing at all.'

'He's told you about Megan, right?' Luke said to Marcus Pollack. 'Mike's let you know that she's still alive? That's our trump card here, but I wasn't sure when to play it.'

Pollack furrowed his brow. 'I'm going to pretend that I didn't hear that,' he said. 'Your sister is being buried in London in a few days' time. After that, anyone who claims to be her will have a great deal of difficulty proving their identity. Legally, you will be the only child of Jack Kite, and the inheritor of the majority of his considerable estate.'

Luke looked at the lawyer in dismay. Marcus Pollack was part of the plan to get rid of Megan. Of course he was. And, in a sense, Luke was, too. Everybody thought that he should disown his half-sister. It would make his life so much easier. And Megan really had vanished. Maybe she was already dead. If Luke told the police what he knew, they would be unable to find her. She wasn't his problem. Getting out of custody was.

'OK,' he said, 'what do you suggest I do?'

'Nothing. You plan to attend your sister's funeral, yes?'

'Of course.'

'Then let me do the talking.'

Pollack went out briefly, then brought Trevelyan back in.

'My client has nothing to hide and is anxious to return to London to attend his sister's funeral,' he said. 'I, on behalf of Kite Industries, volunteer to travel to the UK with him and guarantee that Lucas Kite is available for interview at any time other than the day of the funeral. There will, therefore, be no need for any kind of extradition order. Luke is as anxious as you are to solve the murders of his sister and his friend's sister. But he is also anxious to go home to his mother and prepare for his sister's funeral.'

Trevelyan seemed surprised by the offer. 'You'll give me that assurance in writing? With full details of when he's travelling and where he's staying at all times?'

'You have my word,' Marcus Pollack said.

'Deal.'

The two men shook hands on it.

TOKYO

Outside the Mori tower in Roppongi Hills was an enormous bronze spider by the sculptor Louise Bourgeois, just like one Megan had seen at the Tate Modern when she was a kid. Seeing it reminded her of good times with Mum and Dad. She wished Dad were there to recall them with her.

The first six floors of the tower were a luxurious shopping mall. Megan had checked out the mall earlier – not to buy stuff, but to suss out escape routes and make sure she wasn't being followed. She needed to be able to get away quickly if need be. She could take the lift down to the fourth floor and drift through different stores before sneaking to the station.

The Tokyo City View observation deck was a good place to meet, except that you had to pay to get in to the viewing area and it used up most of Megan's money. She hadn't had the chance to take out any more yen with Grace's cash card.

Most visitors were clustered around the vast windows, taking in the panorama of Tokyo, an uncountable number of huge buildings. The distant ones seemed to get taller as they faded into a haze of smog. From here, the city could be the world's largest collection of Lego models. A very tall structure was opposite her. It looked like a copy of the Eiffel tower, but in red. Megan scanned the viewing area. There was Toru, in one of the armchairs by the big windows. Megan took off her face mask and sat down next to him. Only then did Toru realize who she was.

'You have dyed your hair. Excellent disguise!'

'Thank you.'

'Once I am sure you have not been followed, I will take you to your father.'

'Really?' Megan could hardly contain her excitement. She had been feeling so alone for so long. All that was about to change.

Toru looked over her shoulder. He seemed nervous. His life must be in danger, too.

'What I don't understand,' Megan said, 'is why Dad's pretending to be dead. Presumably the helicopter crash wasn't an accident?'

'His helicopter was shot down, I believe.'

'But now that he's safe, surely Dad has the means to

188

protect himself against whoever's after him?'

Toru nodded vigorously. 'Indeed he does, but your father wishes to exploit the situation, to draw his enemies out.'

'And by enemies, who do you mean?'

Toru didn't reply, so Megan pressed the point.

'I need to know. Is it my uncle? Or are my enemies the terrorists who first claimed responsibility for Dad's death? You know my uncle, don't you? He mentioned you.'

Toru nodded. A lucky guess. Megan looked out of the window, where a large helicopter was flying by. It would be easy for a terrorist to pick her off here, Megan realized. A rocket or a bomb from outside would be a spectacular way to kill her, with a few hundred other people as collateral damage. Maybe Toru was conscious of that, too. Maybe that was why he seemed so nervous. He kept checking his phone. A text arrived and he gave a tight smile.

'I knew your uncle when he worked in Tokyo, yes. Very nice man. Your father will answer all of your questions when I take you to him. Now, please follow me.'

'Sure.' They left the viewing platform and got into the lift. They were alone, so Megan was able to ask another question that was preying on her mind.

'Dad loves his company so much, I'm surprised he's let the stock drop so badly. A lot of his investors have lost out.'

'But not him,' Toru said. 'Falling stock price allowed your father to boost his holding considerably when it reached bottom. He now owns even more of Kite Industries than he did before.'

'And the stock price will rise again when he reveals that he's still alive,' Megan said.

'Exactly!' Toru clapped his hands together in delight.

Megan pulled on her face mask to hide her expression. Dad would never play with people's livelihoods like that. He was ambitious and competitive, but not greedy, not deceitful. For him, money was just a way of keeping score, a means to an end. He gave away more than he spent on himself, although, unlike most businessmen, he didn't show off about it. Megan only knew because she used to help him choose the charities to give to. So, whoever Toru had been talking with, it wasn't Dad.

The lift reached the ground. Megan knew what she was going to see before the door opened.

'Thank you, Toru,' said the balding American in the safari suit. Before Megan could run, Toru grabbed her right arm and the American took her left. Between them, they lifted her from the ground. Megan screamed, but it was no use. The waiting car was only a few metres away, its windows shaded.

'Nice disguise,' said the American. 'Very helpful. Sexist society you have here. Nobody cares what happens to local girls. A white girl might have roused their interest.'

He pushed Megan into the open rear passenger door, then got in beside her. Toru took the front passenger side. The car set off. Megan was, for the first time in her life, terrified.

She was sure of two things. Her father really was dead. And soon she would be, too.

Thirty

TOKYO

Megan sat between Toru and Safari Suit. None of them wore seat belts. She was not restrained but had heard the click of the doors locking as she got in. Against her side Megan could feel the hard lump of metal stored under Safari Suit's left shoulder.

The large car with the shaded windows made steady progress through an unfamiliar part of Tokyo. The man in the safari suit answered his mobile. He'd made a short, terse call almost as soon as they got in the car. His tone this time was more polite. If Megan leaned to her left a little, she could hear the caller. The accent was American, with the odd English inflection. Uncle Mike.

'. . . die in a road accident. The important thing is that the body's not traceable. It needs to be covered in lime and buried or weighed down and dropped out at sea. Got that, Jimmy?'

'Got it. Plenty of building sites we can use.'

Megan shivered. Her uncle and her assassin were discussing her death. There was no longer any need for secrecy. She had nothing to lose. Megan prodded her captor.

191

'Let me speak to him.'

The balding man ignored her.

'Shut her up,' he told Toru.

Toru twisted his arm around Megan's mouth but she shook it away.

'Get off me!' she shouted. 'Let me speak to my uncle. If he's ordering my death, let him at least explain himself.'

The assassin ignored her, continuing his conversation. 'Sorry about that. What? You're sure? OK.'

Safari Suit gave Megan a sneering glance then handed her the phone. 'Don't try anything.'

Megan snatched the phone from him. 'Mike?'

'Hello Megan.' Her uncle's voice was as smooth and confident as ever.

'Why are you doing this?'

'It's nothing personal, Megan.'

'Nothing personal? My dad is dead, isn't he?'

'Jack died in the helicopter crash, yes.'

Megan had to get him talking. She had half a plan. And if she was about to die, she might as well get some answers.

'But it wasn't an accident?'

'It could have been an accident. Jack wasn't a good enough pilot to fly solo, but he was always an arrogant son of a . . .'

'Was the guy sitting next to me behind it?'

'No, Jimmy's in charge of our Eastern operation. Graham Palmer fired that missile.'

'Was Palmer the guy who tried to run me over?'

'Yes. He was less successful when he ran over your friend by mistake, then missed you in Krakow. We were in a rush, but things should have been more professionally done.'

Megan struggled to take in what her uncle was confessing to her. Such honesty made it certain that he was about to have her killed.

'Why did you have to act quickly? What did Dad do?'

'Jack found out about the software I'd had developed for detonating chemical weapons. He was on the verge of sacking me.'

'There was no terrorist threat?'

'Of course not. If there'd been time, I'd have made the terrorist group more convincing. And I'd have found a more subtle way to get you out of the picture. But that's enough questions. Goodbye, Megan. Return the phone to Mr Quigley.'

'Hold on,' Megan said, keeping one eye focused outside the car window. 'Is Luke in this with you?'

'Of course he is,' Mike replied. 'Luke and I are very close.'

'So he blew up his own apartment to make it look like . . .'

'Precisely. The explosion was designed to keep suspicion away from him.'

Megan didn't know what else to say. They were about to join a motorway that led out of the city. Once they were on it, Megan would have no chance to stop the car and attract help. How could she distract the driver and other passengers? Oh, the hell with it. She played for time.

'Who was that poor girl who was killed in the Barbican? How are you managing to have her buried instead of me?'

'Her parents took some convincing,' Mike gloated. 'But we explained that your appearing to be dead was the only way to keep you safe. And we gave them a very large amount of money to help with their grief.'

The conversation had been going on so long that Toru had relaxed his grip on her. Jimmy the assassin leaned forward to say something to the driver.

'I see,' Megan said. 'Tell me one last thing . . .'

The car picked up speed. The driver turned the wheel. Any moment now. Megan pressed her feet hard against the floor. Her body had to be a coiled spring. The car entered the ramp that curved down on to the motorway. Now.

Megan propelled herself between the front seats of the car. She bashed against the driver. He looked round, confused. Megan grabbed the wheel and twisted it so that the car kept turning. She felt one of the men in the back grab her left foot. She kicked hard and pulled the foot free.

'You're dead!' threatened the balding American.

Megan let go of the steering wheel. The whole of her body was in the front of the car now, first tumbling against the driver, then thrown to the other side of the car. Jimmy tried to grab her. Before he could, the car crashed into the barrier.

Jimmy was thrown back. Megan banged her head. The car bounced off the barrier. Megan heard an ominous click that she remembered from the times when she had bodyguards. It was the safety-catch-release mechanism of a loaded gun.

The second time the car hit the side of the ramp, the barrier breached. Megan smashed her head on the roof. Two air-bags expanded rapidly, crushing her. She heard Toru scream and the American swear. Then she lost consciousness.

MANHATTAN

Luke was woken by the phone. His mother answered it and kept her voice low, which might mean trouble. He got out of bed as quietly as he could, crept across the room and opened his door a crack. He could make out Mom's end of the conversation.

'That's a relief. They're going to . . . I see. We fly tonight. When are you . . .? OK, I'll tell him. In London, yes. You too.'

Luke wandered into the living area as Mom put down the phone. 'Who was that?' he asked.

'Your uncle, about arrangements for Megan's funeral.'

'Why didn't he talk to me?'

'Because he thought that what I'm going to tell you would come better from me.'

'Which is what?'

'They located your sister.'

'*They?*'

'People your uncle hired. It's not good, Luke.'

'What do you mean?' Luke looked at his mom. Her expression was meant to be sympathetic, but her eyes were empty.

'Megan's dead, Luke. She was killed in a traffic accident in Tokyo, Japan.'

'I know where Tokyo is!' Luke snapped. 'My sister's died twice? I don't believe you. What was she doing in Japan?'

'I don't know and I don't suppose we'll ever find out.'

'She was trying to get away, wasn't she? From Uncle Mike

and his henchmen.'

'Don't be so melodramatic,' Crystal told him.

'My sister's dead, for no reason. That's pretty dramatic as far as I'm concerned.'

'There are never reasons for road accidents. A moment's carelessness is all it takes. Megan was unlucky.'

Luke sat down and put his head in his hands. 'At least this gets the police off my back,' he said, after a while. 'They can hardly accuse me of flying to Tokyo and running her over. I was in custody until nine hours ago.'

Mom didn't reply. Luke was used to reading her silences.

'What?' he demanded.

'We can't tell the police that Megan died in Japan.'

So they had killed her, Luke was certain. On his behalf.

'There's no evidence you had anything to do with what happened in London,' Crystal went on. 'Don't worry about that.'

'OK,' Luke said, quietly. 'But what about her body?'

'That won't be an issue. Your uncle will fix it. Anything's possible when you have money. Her funeral's in two days' time. Let's make it a good occasion. It'll be for the best in the long run, believe me.'

Thirty-One

TOKYO

Megan didn't know where she was. Her side hurt. Somebody spoke Japanese to her. Couldn't they tell she was English? She opened her eyes. This was a hospital.

'I want to leave,' she said.

The nurse said some more stuff in Japanese. Megan got out of the bed. At least they had put her in a room of her own, not a public ward or, worse, an operating theatre.

'Where are my clothes?' she asked.

The nurse made a gesture which indicated that Megan should get back into bed. Megan ignored her. She ached in several places. It didn't feel like any bones were broken. She had to go. She had to get out of here before Jimmy Quigley got to her again. There was a small cupboard by her bed and her clothes were in it. So was her knapsack, which had been in the back of the car. And the phone she had been using just before the crash. It said the time was just after seven. Her flight to Sydney left at ten. If she didn't leave now, she would miss it. Maybe it was already too late. How near the airport was she?

Megan put the mobile in the knapsack and dressed as

quickly as she could. She was really stiff, so was still buttoning up her shirt when the nurse returned. With her was a doctor who didn't look much older than Megan.

'You are very lucky to be alive,' he said.

'Good old air-bags,' Megan replied.

'The air-bags protected you, but not in the way that they were designed to. They did not save the driver. He broke his neck. The passengers in the back seat might have lived, had they worn seat belts. You were lucky, for you were not wearing a seat belt either.'

'There was a reason for that,' Megan said. 'Do you want to hear it?'

She had to level with someone, though she doubted this guy would welcome the truth. Once you knew the situation, you were involved. The doctor didn't let her tell the story.

'We had to cut your shirt off. Two of your ribs are cracked.'

'Listen, there are people trying to kill me.'

'I see,' the doctor said, stroking his chin. 'We have very good police. They will want to talk to you.'

'It's not so straightforward,' Megan told the doctor. 'These are very rich people. They can afford to buy the police. They will try to buy you.'

'Not everyone can be bought,' the doctor told her.

'People who can't be bought can be killed. These are very powerful, very dangerous people.'

The doctor lowered his head so that she couldn't see his eyes.

'I understand.'

'You don't sound too surprised.'

'The paramedics found a gun in the car. We often deal with gang shootings here. After a while, not much surprises you.'

'Listen.' Megan lowered her voice. 'Can you tell anyone who asks after me that I'm dead?'

'Why?'

'Because if you don't, they will find a way to kill me.'

'I'm afraid I can't do that. You are here. There is no body.'

'I'm not talking about lying to the police, I'm talking about people from Kite Industries, particularly a man called Graham Palmer. These people want to kill me. If they come, please tell them that I broke my neck, too. Tell them my body was thrown from the car and you don't know where it was taken. That'll give me time to get away. I have a plane ticket in my pocket. I can be out of Japan in a few hours. Another country's problem.'

Again, the doctor hesitated.

'Please, you'd be saving my life.'

He considered. 'I can't stop you discharging yourself. I will not tell lies, but I will not talk to anybody from outside the hospital about you. That is the best I can offer.'

'Thank you.' Megan thought for a moment. 'I don't know where I am. How do I get to the airport from here?'

'Wait.' The doctor spoke to the nurse, who hurried away. 'We are near to Narita airport. I will have an ambulance take you there. You will go in a wheelchair, yes?'

'Yes. Thank you. Thank you so much.'

'I do not want violence here. But we must act quickly. You have been unconscious for two hours. The gun I told you about, it is already gone. Somebody paid somebody to remove it. And our police are not here yet, which is not right. For us, perhaps, it would be safest if you were never in this hospital.'

'I was never in this country,' Megan said, as the nurse returned with the wheelchair.

'OK. Good luck, Miss Thompson.'

Megan leaned over and kissed him on the cheek.

'If anybody makes you tell them about me,' she said, 'don't say my name is Thompson. Tell them I said my name was Kite, Megan Kite.'

'The men who died worked for a company called Kite.'

'Yes,' Megan said. 'I know.'

HEATHROW

Grace accompanied her brother to the airport, substituting her crutches with a walking stick. She would have flown to Sydney herself, but she'd miss the funeral. Also, there was no way she could make such a long journey without further messing up her legs. Ethan had protested about what she was asking him to do. As they stood outside Departures, he remained unconvinced.

'This could be a colossal waste of time and money,' Ethan said. 'I'll get there after Megan. She'll have several hours' start.'

'She's bound to get in touch,' Grace assured him.

'Not necessarily.'

'She will. Then I'll let her know where you are. You can

take her to the British Embassy, get them to phone Mum. Once our government believes that she's really alive, the authorities can take it from there.'

'And if they don't believe either of us?'

'They have to. You're a government minister's son.'

The tannoy gave the final call for Ethan's flight. 'I'd like to hear you explain to Mum and Dad why I've flown to Sydney to go surfing on Bondi beach when it's the end of winter there.'

'They'll think you got the seasons mixed up.'

'They might think you're that stupid, but not me. Wish me luck.'

She kissed her brother on the cheek. 'Give Megan my love. You'll find her. I know you will.'

LONDON

Luke let himself into his father's Barbican flat. The crime scene tape was long gone. Cleaners had done a thorough job. The rooms were aired. No bloodstains. No messages on the answering machine either. It had been disconnected.

This place was his now. In trust until he was eighteen, but he could move in today if he wanted. Luke had always loved this penthouse, with its swish, hi-tech fittings and fantastic view. Dad had owned it for seven years, but this was only Luke's third visit. He walked round the airy, spacious flat, opening doors and looking in drawers. In Dad's bedroom were three big photos of Megan and a small one of Luke. Said it all.

The phone rang. Luke hesitated, then answered it. Mike.

'How's it going? Did they clean the place? I asked the service to sort you out some closet space and put a few essentials in the fridge. You should be good for a few days.'

'It's fine. I'm just settling in.'

'Your mother with you?'

'No, she said that staying here after the murders would be too creepy. She's in the same Bloomsbury hotel we used before.'

'You don't want to be with her?'

'To be honest, Mike, I can use the space at the moment.'

'Sure. I understand.'

Luke began the hardest question. 'About the car accident in Tokyo . . .'

'She told you about that?'

'Do you have any details?'

'Not much. All of the people who died worked for me. I don't know what your sister was running away from, Luke. But you have to move beyond the tragedies. Start again.'

'When do you get here?'

'The evening before the funeral.'

'Where will you stay?'

'Same place as your mom, I figure. She could probably do with some company.'

'That's good of you. I know Mom can be . . . difficult sometimes. I appreciate how you look after her.'

'I like difficult women,' Mike said. 'More of a challenge.'

'Bull.' Luke laughed half-heartedly. He didn't appreciate Mike acting like fancied his mom, not even in jest.

'Gotta go,' Mike said. 'See you in a couple of days.'

Luke turned on the wall-mounted TV and muted it, waiting for the story about a car crash in Tokyo to come round. He stared at the screen, but his mind was elsewhere. He had to work out who he was and who he wanted to be.

Luke was his mother's son. An accident. No wonder Jack Kite didn't have much time for him. How much did Luke take from his father, how much from his mother? You got more of your personality from the person who brought you up, didn't you? Jack Kite wasn't a real dad. Luke didn't miss him much. He'd missed Jack more when he was still alive.

Soon, Luke would have something more valuable than his father's love. His money. He could be whoever and whatever he chose to be. Megan's death, deliberate or accidental, gave Luke that freedom. All he had lost was a half-sister he only saw for a few days a year: that was how Mike saw it. Let him think Luke was as greedy as he was. Luke could hardly wait to see Mike and Crystal's reaction when he turned eighteen and signed over the whole lot to whichever Third World charity took his fancy.

Luke saw his surname on the TV so turned up the sound.

'Accidents continue to stalk software giant Kite Industries. One of Kite's security officers, James Quigley, along with a driver and a Japanese interpreter, Toru Suzuki, were killed when their car crashed through the barrier on an entrance ramp yesterday evening. Japanese police are examining the wreckage of the car in order to determine the cause of the accident.'

No mention of Megan. Uncle Mike had erased her second death as completely as he had faked her first.

Thirty-Two

TOKYO

The flight to Sydney was delayed because of bad weather. Megan spent a nervous extra hour in the airport, expecting to be found by her uncle's henchmen. Mike must know by now that she was still alive. At midnight, she was allowed to board the plane. She should be OK, she told herself. As long as the hospital doctor kept his word and nobody knew that she was travelling as Grace Thompson. In ten hours' time, she would be in Sydney, an English-speaking city. She could disappear until her eighteenth birthday or beyond.

What lay beyond? She was already dead. For Megan to prove she wasn't would be difficult – impossible, maybe, when she wasn't on any DNA database and her closest relatives were willing to lie about who she was. Her only solution would be to return where people knew her. But that would mean returning to the people who had already tried to kill her three times.

The plane began to taxi along the runway. Megan checked the in-flight movies. She had been asleep, by her calculation, for the best part of fourteen hours in the last twenty-four. It was unlikely that she would doze off again.

She needed a thriller, or, failing that, some kind of romance she could get sucked into.

There was an announcement in Japanese. The plane juddered to a stop. The announcement was repeated in English. 'A red light has come on in the cockpit, so we must return to the airport in order to locate the problem.'

They taxied back to Narita airport. The other passengers, mostly Japanese with a smattering of Australians, took it stoically. Better safe than sorry. But Megan felt herself begin to panic. Her enemies knew she was on the plane. This was deliberate. Somebody was coming to get her. When the passengers were forced to get off, they would be waiting for her.

But nobody got off the plane. After three-quarters of an hour, the pilot announced that they had still not located the problem. He was being forced to turn off the air-conditioning at the rear, where Megan was sitting, so that technicians could strip one of the engines. Megan could hear some of the Aussies complaining that they ought to be taken off the plane and allocated another. Megan knew better. She'd talked with Dad about Kite's latest air flight management programs. She knew there wouldn't be a plane available without disrupting endless other flight schedules.

A meal was served, without alcohol, and the in-flight entertainment was turned on. A steward apologized that, because they weren't in the air, the system wasn't fully operational. She was right. All of the movies seemed to have started in the middle and neither the rewind nor fast forward buttons worked. Megan chose a silly comedy she'd watched with Grace, earlier in the year. At least she knew the story.

The air-conditioning was only off for three-quarters of an hour, but that was long enough for Megan to get sticky and sweaty. Her painkillers were starting to wear off. By the time a second movie ended, the plane had been delayed for four hours. At least Megan could be sure the engine problem was genuine, not a pretext to get her off the plane. After five hours, the pilot announced that the engine had been stripped and rebuilt, and they would be ready to set off in thirty minutes or so. 'Unless the red light reappears. Should this occur, I'm afraid, we won't be going anywhere tonight.'

In the seats ahead of Megan, an Australian couple discussed what it would be like to be taken to the airport Holiday Inn at four in the morning. For the second time that night, the plane began to taxi along the runway. At the point where, previously, the jet had slowed down, it accelerated, then rose smoothly into the air. A few people applauded. Megan was not among them. She was so relieved that she fell into a deep, dreamless sleep, and would not wake until the plane began to descend towards Sydney, nine hours later.

SCOTLAND

The sleeper train to Edinburgh was cramped and uncomfortable, but the highlands view the next morning was spectacular. Luke had trouble persuading the taxi driver that he really wanted to go all the way to Brunts school.

'Here, look!' Luke flashed the stash of cash he had found in Dad's safe. 'And I'll only be there for an hour or two, so if you hang around, I've got to make a brief hospital visit, then

I'll need driving to the airport.'

He'd taken the train here because plane journeys were easy to trace, whereas security on trains was minimal. Luke's uncle had eyes everywhere. Once they were well on their way, Luke rang the school and told the Head that he was coming to collect his sister's stuff.

'There's no need for you to do it in person,' Mrs Duncan said. 'I could have arranged to have it delivered to London.'

'I'm in the area,' Luke said, 'but I'm flying home, so I'll probably only take the light, more valuable things. Maybe you can have the rest delivered to me.'

'Fine. I'll see you in . . . ?'

Luke leaned forward to the driver. 'How long?'

The man opened and closed his left hand three times.

'I'll be there in fifteen minutes,' Luke said.

Megan's school was less palatial than Luke had been expecting, but somehow more impressive. It was one of the oldest in Scotland and had abundant grounds, set well back from the nearby main road. When the guard at the gate let the taxi through, they could have been entering another century. Luke's Brooklyn middle school looked like a prison camp in comparison. The architecture reminded Luke of London's Houses of Parliament. What was the word for the style? Dad had told him once. Gothic.

Mrs Duncan met him at the school steps.

'Would you like to see my passport?' Luke offered. He had come prepared to prove who he was.

'No need. I've seen your picture many times,' Mrs Duncan said. 'Megan has a photograph of you in her room.

'Please accept all of our condolences. Megan was a wonderful young woman. To lose both her and your father in such a short space of time must have been a terrible blow to you.'

'Terrible,' Luke agreed, examining the Head's face for any traces of suspicion. He was the man with the motive, after all.

'Let me take you straight to her room.'

It was nearly the end of term, the Head explained. The Year Eleven and Thirteen girls were long gone. 'I expect you heard about the accident that befell Megan's room-mate.'

'I did. How is she?'

'Much better. They let her out of hospital two days ago.'

'Grace Thompson's back in London? I was hoping to visit her before the funeral.'

'I'm sure I can find you a contact number. When is the funeral?'

'The day after tomorrow.'

'That's very short notice,' Mrs Duncan observed.

'I'm sorry. My uncle's been handling all the arrangements and invitations. But he's had a load on his mind.'

The corridors smelled of wood polish, fresh flowers and faint, expensive deodorant. The smell of privilege. Seeing this place told Luke a lot about Megan.

'This is . . . was your sister's room, the one she shared with Grace. Perhaps you'd like to be left here for a while.'

'Thanks.'

Luke waited until the Head's footsteps receded. Then he had a good root around. He didn't know what he was looking for, but he would know it when he found it. Megan had lots of clothes. No point in having those sent on. Did they have Goodwill in Scotland, he wondered? They must have some kind of charity shops here, no matter how rich the area. He couldn't find any diaries or an electronic organizer. In Brooklyn, he dimly recalled, Megan had complained about leaving here in a hurry, not having all her stuff with her. There must be more than he could see. A-ha! At the back of the wardrobe was a small iron safe. A simple one, like you got in hotels. All Luke had to do was figure out the combination. He set to work.

It had been easy, yesterday, to unlock his dad's safe. Luke knew all the significant names and numbers in his dad's life. Guessing the right ones took less than five minutes. But this combination was numbers only and, chances were, Megan shared it with Grace Thompson. Luke knew next to nothing about Grace, except that she was a cabinet minister's daughter. He found his way to the Head's office. Mrs Duncan looked up.

'There's also your sister's bicycle . . .'

'Please send it to the London flat. Listen. There's a safe in the room. I don't suppose you have the combination?'

'I'm afraid not,' Mrs Duncan said. 'Several of the girls have safes but it's a private matter and they always take them away at the end of their time with us.'

'Is it possible her room-mate has the combination, that they shared it?'

'Yes, it's quite possible. Let me get you her number.'

Luke put the number into his phone. He returned to the room before he rang Grace. If she didn't answer, this would have been a wasted journey. But she did. Luke explained who he was and her voice became more tentative.

'Eh . . . Luke, hi. I'm so sorry for your loss.'

'I'm at Brunts, sorting out some of Megan's things.'

'I see.'

'There's a safe here. I think you shared it with Megan.'

'Of course, yes, I'd forgotten about the safe.'

'It's locked. Can you tell me the combination?'

'Um . . .'

The line went quiet. If Luke was in Grace's position, he wouldn't want anybody else looking in his safe either. But he had to get to the bottom of what had happened to his sister. He had to do a risk assessment before he got to the funeral.

'I realize you might have some private stuff in there, but I promise only to look at stuff that belongs to my sister.'

'There's a journal I'd rather you didn't look at. I was hoping my parents would get it when they collected my clothes but I couldn't remember the combination then, either. Megan's diary may be there, too. She didn't keep it all that often. I don't know what she took with her. I'm sorry . . .'

'Take your time,' Luke said.

'I want to help. It's just that I'm useless with numbers. I had it written down somewhere. I'm trying to remember . . .'

She was playing for time. Luke tried his last card. 'The thing is, the funeral's only two days away and I'm not going to be able to get to Scotland again before I go home. Anything that'll help me understand Megan and what happened to her . . .'

'I can tell you that it's a combination of our birthdays,' Grace said, 'but I can't remember the order.'

'Tell me your birthday and I'll work it out from there.'
She told him.

'OK,' Luke said. 'I'll call you back if I get stuck.'

He hung up the phone before she could reply and had the door open in less than a minute. He pulled out the two journals first of all, and opened his sister's. The handwriting was wrong, but that made no sense, as it had her photo pasted on the cover. No, wait. He looked at the photo again. Not Megan, so this must be Grace. The two girls were so close they had the same hairstyle. Luke put Megan's diary in his pocket to read on the plane. There was some jewellery. He didn't know which was Megan's and which was Grace's, so he took it all. And there was a large wallet. Should he take that to give to Grace in London? He opened it to see what was inside. It wasn't Grace's. This was his sister's wallet, which contained her credit cards, even her passport. But if her passport was here, how had she got to New York? And out again? He could only think of one solution. No wonder Mike had had such trouble tracking her.

Thirty-Three

SYDNEY

You weren't allowed to use mobile phones until you were through Customs, but plenty of people were checking theirs, so Megan got out the one that used to belong to Luke. He had told her that it didn't work in London, so she wasn't expecting it to work here, with its Polish SIM card. It didn't. All the phone told her was the time: seven in the morning in Krakow, which meant it was three in the afternoon in Tokyo and an hour later in Sydney.

Megan had a second phone, the one that belonged to Jimmy Quigley. It was too dangerous to turn that one on. If Kite Industries knew she had the phone, someone there might get an alert as soon as the phone connected to a satellite. They'd be able to locate her.

Kite Industries probably had an office in Sydney. In a fairer world, Megan would be able to go there and sort everything out. *She* was meant to be the boss, not her uncle. But Megan didn't feel anything like a boss. She felt like a hapless schoolgirl, way out of her depth. She got to the front of the immigration queue and handed over her passport. The immigration officer scanned the passport through a card reader and something beeped. A stern, bulky woman pushed her glasses down her nose and stared at Megan.

'Grace Thompson?'

'Yes.'

'Full UK citizen?'

'Yes.'

'Date of birth?'

Megan reeled off the details of her best friend's birthday. She hadn't been asked anything like this when she entered Japan, Poland or the USA.

'Your hair's dyed, right?'

'Oh, yes, of course. I had it done in Japan.'

'I see.'

Meg had forgotten that she looked so different. Earlier, her hairstyle and colour had made Megan a near ringer for Grace, as long as you didn't look too closely. She guessed what the machine's beep meant. A face didn't match a passport photo. Some airports had started using biometric facial recognitions software. Megan knew about the software's potential. Kite Industries was developing facial recognition systems. They accessed the electronic copy of the passport photo kept in the passport's computer chip, then checked it against one taken by a face scanner in the airport. Megan should have considered this possibility before, but there was nothing she could do to thwart it now.

'Come with me, please.'

Two uniformed immigration officers appeared and, before Megan could protest, escorted her to a grey office.

'Wait here until an officer is free to interview you.'

They locked the door and left her to stew.

LONDON

Grace couldn't sleep. It was light enough for her to read her bedside clock. Just gone six. That must make it four or five in the afternoon in Sydney. Grace needed to call Ethan. Luke would have worked out by now that Megan was travelling under Grace's passport. She must be told. Why hadn't Grace kept quiet about the safe combination? It might be days before Ethan found her friend. Nevertheless, she decided to leave a message. It would be waiting for Ethan when he landed.

She could use a cup of tea before stringing words together in any semblance of meaning. Grace dragged herself out of bed and pulled on her dressing gown. Her injuries were fading but she still ached a lot, especially first thing. From her parents' room, she heard a telephone ring. Early, even for them. Descending the hall stairs, she heard her mum's voice.

'Yes, she's here. Starting to get about on crutches, but the funeral will be the first time she's left the house. Can you hold off replying to them, though? I need to find something out first.'

Grace put water in the kettle, turned it on. She put two bags in the pot, then, hearing footsteps, added a third. Mum joined her in the kitchen.

'Can never get back to sleep after an early morning call.'

'What was it about?'

'A girl just showed up at Sydney airport, using your passport, and claiming to be you. But she didn't pass their facial scan software. UK Immigration has been contacted. They recognized the name, so they contacted me just now, wanting to know if this girl really is my daughter.'

'Ah,' Grace said. 'What did you tell them?'

'*Ah* indeed. I told them not to respond until I'd checked a few things out.'

'There's something I'd better tell you,' Grace said.

SYDNEY

There were two of them and they scared Megan, but not as much as she'd been scared by the people who'd tried to kill her. The guy who took the lead was fortyish, suited and suntanned.

'Travelling under false documents is a serious offence.'

'I keep telling you, your software's faulty.'

'Miss whoever-you-are, you bear only a slight resemblance to the photograph in your passport. Your nose is wrong. Your eyes are a different shape. Your chin is more pointed.'

'It's a bad photograph.'

'Who are you?'

Megan was tempted to make a bad joke. *I could tell you the answer, but then someone would try to kill you.* 'I've told you who I am.'

Maybe she was playing this wrong. Tell them the truth and the Australians would get her to the authorities, protect her. But what if, when she told them that she was really a dead person, they had her committed to a psychiatric ward?

'Let's try a different tack. What are you doing in Australia?'

'Holiday. I just finished my exams.'

The older one of her interrogators glanced at his pager and left the room, leaving Megan with a woman in her late twenties. She had been quiet so far. The woman leaned forward.

'Tell me, Grace.' She leaned forward and smiled. 'Can I call you "Grace"?' Meg nodded. 'Why did you dye your hair?'

So that was it: they were playing 'good cop, bad cop'.

'I was fed up of people staring at my hair in Tokyo. I get very self-conscious.'

'But you were only in Tokyo for two or three nights.'

'It was an impulse. It didn't occur to me that I'd create this kind of a problem, and I'm sorry.'

The woman tapped away at her laptop. 'Would there be any images of you on the net that would make it easier for me to positively identify you?'

'Not that I'm aware of, sorry.' But type in *Megan Kite* and you'd get a bit of a shock, Megan thought. Luckily, Grace's parents were protective of her privacy. The Thompsons kept Grace and Ethan out of the public eye. There were no loving family publicity shots online. Megan hadn't yet revealed that her 'mother' was a cabinet minister. That would make the situation even more complicated.

Her other interrogator returned.

'We've checked your entry and exit records from the US. Your fingerprints match the ones given on entry.'

'Great,' Megan said. 'Does that prove that I am who I am?'

'No, it only proves that you're the same person who left London several days ago.'

'Then what should I do?' Megan asked.

'We're trying to verify your details with UK Immigration. In the meantime, is there anyone in Australia who can vouch for you?' the woman asked. 'Somebody you're staying with, perhaps?'

Megan shook her head.

'Is there a family member we could call?' Suntan wanted to know. 'Somebody who might be able to provide us with convincing proof of your identity. Parents? Siblings?'

'Sure,' Megan said, stalling. She didn't want these guys calling the cabinet minister, or her husband, the Euro MP. Plus, she didn't have phone numbers for Grace's parents. But she did have one number that might do the job.

'There's my elder brother, Ethan,' she said. 'I've got his number on my phone. But I'm unclear what time of day it is in the UK. He's not exactly an early riser.'

'Let's see, shall we?' said the woman, with a brisk smile.

Megan found the number in her contacts list. The immigration officer tapped it into her own mobile. There was a short delay as the call was routed around the world.

'Mr Thompson. This is Nicola Robinson from the Australian Department of Immigration and Citizenship. I have a woman here who's travelling on your sister's passport but is otherwise unable to prove her identity. Do you know where your sister is?'

Pause.

'I see. And where are you at the moment, Mr Thompson?'

Brief pause.

'Right. OK. Wait for me. I'll come and get you now.'

She put down the phone and snarled at Megan, all trace of good cop gone. 'Why didn't you tell us your brother was joining you here and could vouch for you? Do you take us for fools?'

'You never asked,' Megan said, trying to hide her surprise. What the hell was Ethan doing in Sydney?

Thirty-Four

LONDON

Luke was on his way out of the Barbican when they arrested him again. Two uniforms stopped him at the door, handcuffed him, bundled him into a car and took him to Scotland Yard. Ian Trevelyan from Special Branch was waiting there.

'Where's my lawyer?' Luke asked. 'I thought you had a deal with Marcus.'

'Mr Pollack hasn't landed in the UK yet. I believe he flies today. He was supposed to be accompanying you. But you chose to come here early. I wonder why.'

'I had some stuff to sort out.'

Trevelyan waited for Luke to elaborate but Luke added nothing. Marcus had advised Luke on how to deal with cops. Never give more information than the minimum they ask for.

'You went to Scotland, I believe. What was so important that you had to visit your sister's school in person?'

They thought that Megan died in London, Luke reminded himself. He couldn't explain that he was looking for clues about her second death, in Japan. He couldn't explain much at all.

'I went to collect her stuff. There was a safe. I wanted to get into it.'

'And what did you find?'

'Nothing important. I'm not certain what belonged to her and what belonged to her room-mate, who had a bad accident. I was on my way to Grace Thompson's when you picked me up.'

'The minister's daughter?'

'Yes.'

'That'll have to wait, I'm afraid. I have a few more questions for you about your father's death.'

'I don't understand. I was on a different continent when the accident took place.'

'There was no accident,' Trevelyan told Luke, examining his face closely for a reaction to what he said next. 'Your father was murdered. We've recovered fragments from the wreckage which clearly demonstrate that his helicopter was shot down by a hand-fired surface-to-air missile over the North Sea.'

'No!' The word just slipped out.

'There isn't any doubt,' Trevelyan told him. 'So we have to look at who benefits from the murder. Your sister, in the first place. She would have inherited had she survived until her eighteenth birthday. But, with her death, a majority of Kite Industries shares end up going to you.'

'Do I look like the sort of guy who could organize the shooting down of his own father?'

'I don't suppose you acted alone, Luke. Perhaps your uncle had a grudge against his younger brother, with him being so much more successful. Or your mother could be behind this. She must have resented the way your dad used, then dumped her. Your mother's your only alibi for the time when Megan was killed, isn't she? And, even then, the times don't quite add up.'

'This is ridiculous,' Luke insisted. 'I didn't know what was in the will and I didn't kill my sister.'

'Then who did?'

'Give me a moment.'

It was time to choose sides. Luke wanted to avenge Megan's death, not be accused of causing it. Once he told Trevelyan the truth, there was no going back. It meant losing a fortune. He didn't mind that. He'd planned to give it away. It also meant breaking with Mom and Mike for good.

'Who killed Megan?' Trevelyan repeated.

'I don't know, but I'll tell you something, as long as you promise that you won't reveal where you got the information.'

'That depends on the information.'

'I don't want my uncle or mother knowing that I told you. Not yet anyway. And that goes for Marcus Pollack, too.'

Trevelyan looked intrigued. He considered for a moment.

'Very well. Whatever this is, if I need to bring it to the attention of the people you mention, I'll make sure that it appears to come from somewhere else.'

Luke spoke slowly. 'My uncle identified the body in the Barbican as my sister, but it wasn't Megan. It was somebody who happened to be in the wrong place at the wrong time. Mike's paid her family a lot of money to keep quiet about the tragedy.'

Trevelyan didn't seem terribly surprised. 'Who else is aware of this, apart from your uncle?'

'The killer, my mother maybe, and possibly a security guy from Kite Industries, Tom something. Or he may have been the killer, I'm not sure. Megan was meant to be meeting him there.'

'Tom Morris was also killed at the Barbican. We kept that information secret because only the killer would know he was ever in the apartment. Tell me how you know about him?'

'Megan told me. She escaped to New York. But people were after her there, too. I think my friend's sister Maria was killed mistakenly, by someone who thought she was Megan.'

Trevelyan still didn't seem too shocked by what Luke had told him. Or maybe he knew more than he was letting on.

'I'm confused. According to you, is your sister dead or alive?'

Luke hesitated. 'I heard she'd died in a car crash abroad but I'm not sure I trust the person who told me.'

'Your uncle?'

'Yes.'

Trevelyan considered for a moment. 'There's no trace of Megan Kite having left the country.'

'She's not using her own passport.'

'You're sure about that?'

'Certain.' Luke reached into his backpack. 'I have it here.'

SYDNEY

Ethan waited at the baggage reclaim. His phone rang again. He was expecting it to be the Australian immigration officers, but it was his sister.

'Hey. How's it going? I've got news.'

'Me too,' Grace said. 'Mum's just had a call from Special Branch. Megan's dad was definitely murdered.'

Ethan swore.

'Also, Megan's brother Luke rang me. I think he's got into our safe at Brunts. He'll have seen Megan's passport, so he's bound to have worked out by now that she's travelling as me.'

'I've just found Megan,' Ethan told his sister. 'Or at least I'm about to. She's being held in Immigration at Sydney airport. I'm about to go and vouch that she's my sister.'

'That's brilliant. Listen, Mum wants you to bring Megan home.'

'As who? Herself or you? I don't want to get Mum or Megan into any trouble.'

Before Grace could reply, two things happened. Ethan's bag arrived on the carousel and a tall, grey-suited, tanned guy, who could only be an immigration officer, marched towards him. Ethan grabbed his bag and turned his back on the suit. He hung up, then pretended to speak to his mother.

'Mum, I'm just about to go and see Grace, sort things out.'

He turned to face the immigration officer. 'I believe you've found my sister for me.'

'This way please, sir.'

It was a short walk. Ethan was relieved the officer didn't make small talk. He needed to come up with a story, quick. The suit led him into a small interrogation room. Two women sat opposite each other. For a moment, Ethan didn't recognize Megan. She had lost weight and her hair was jet black. When she turned to face him, he knew her, but it was like they were meeting for the first time. She stood. Ethan hurried to her.

'Grace! What have you done to your hair?'

Megan smiled bashfully and hugged Ethan.

'Can we get out of here?' she said, breaking the hug. 'Now?'

'Seriously,' he told her. 'You look great. You ought to keep it that way.'

'Actually, after the trouble I've had here, I was thinking of dying it back to my natural colour as soon as I get to a sink.'

'That might be a while,' Ethan said. 'We need to go back to London.'

'Why?'

Ethan looked over her shoulder. The two immigration officers were following the conversation. They knew that something wasn't right, but Ethan had confirmed his sister's ID and surely they would have no option but to let her go. Still . . . Ethan put on an act.

'There's no easy way to tell you this. Your friend Megan died suddenly. The funeral's tomorrow. I know what a shock this is, but I also know how upset you'd be if you missed the funeral. We need to get on the next plane back to the UK.'

Megan did what anyone would do in the circumstances. She burst into tears and threw herself into Ethan's arms. Embarrassed, the immigration officers sidled out of the room.

'It's OK,' Ethan told her. 'They've gone.'

But she was still crying. Even with her eyes red, obviously dog tired, Ethan thought Megan looked beautiful. He'd never taken her seriously as a potential girlfriend before, for what he now saw was the shallowest of reasons: she looked and dressed too like his sister. Not any more.

After a couple of minutes, Megan pulled away from the hug and asked for a tissue.

'Is it safe for me to go home?' she asked.

'Mum knows you're alive. By the time we get back, we'll have the whole British government working to keep you safe.'

'Multinational corporations can be a lot more powerful than governments,' Megan pointed out.

Ethan hesitated. 'We can stay here if you really want. Australia's a big country. You might be able to stay lost forever. But there's so much money at stake, they'd always be after you. You'd always be looking over your shoulder. Whatever you want, I'll help. But if I were you, I'd go home, front it out.'

Meg still looked doubtful.

'I know that's easy for me to say,' Ethan went on. 'I'm not you. You're probably terrified, with good reason.'

Megan stared at him with her tired, pale eyes.

'I'm too exhausted to be terrified,' she said. 'And you're right, I'm tired of running. I was never intending to stay away forever, only until my eighteenth birthday. I can't let them bury me without a fight. So let's do it. Take me home.'

Thirty-Five

NEW SCOTLAND YARD, LONDON

'You can't attend your own funeral!' Ian Trevelyan, the Special Branch officer said.

'Why not? I've already read my obituaries,' Megan pointed out.

'Because it will give the game away.'

'Only if people recognize me.'

'Which they will, even with your hair dyed.'

'Where is this funeral?'

'Hampstead cemetery. They've chosen a cemetery which has no grave space left, only an area for scattering ashes.'

'So the evidence of my identity will be dust in the wind?'

'It would have been. But the crematorium is under strict instructions not to burn the evidence.'

'And you think my uncle won't find that out?'

Trevelyan shrugged. 'Your uncle's clever, but he's not omniscient. We need to let him inter the dead girl in place of you. It's a vital part of the case against him.'

'What about Luke and Crystal? They're playing along with him.'

'Your brother seems to be cooperating with us. But we

'haven't, of course, told him that you're back in the UK.'

Megan smiled. She'd had her doubts, but always hoped that Luke wasn't against her.

'Luke knows I'm alive?' she checked with Trevelyan.

'No. He thinks you died in Japan. The point is, we don't believe that Luke's in your uncle's pocket. He put us on to the body switch before you reappeared to confirm the story.'

Megan had been back from Australia since early that morning, UK time. She'd been collected from the airport by Special Branch. Special Branch weren't called Special Branch any more. They were part of the Counter Terrorism Unit, but everyone still used the old name. They had been interrogating her all day, apart from a half-hour break in which she'd had a shower and a sandwich.

Earlier, when Ian Trevelyan introduced himself, he'd explained how Special Branch had become involved in Megan's case. They were investigating Kite Industries' claims that terrorists had killed Dad. They'd found no evidence of terrorist activity beyond a few threatening emails, but launched a painstaking hunt for fragments from the helicopter crash. They had just come up with evidence that the crash wasn't an accident.

That wasn't all. According to Trevelyan, a girl called Maria had been murdered in Brooklyn and local law enforcement couldn't figure out the motive. The Brooklyn police had hauled in Megan's brother. Eventually, a story emerged – the poor girl had died because she was mistaken for Megan.

'And you think my uncle was responsible for her death?'

'Thinking something and proving it are two different

matters. Your uncle might be a British subject, but he's got dual nationality and he's hardly ever in our jurisdiction. He flies in by private jet, which is hard to keep track of. We know he'll be in the UK this afternoon because of your funeral. As of now, all we can arrest him for is falsely identifying your body. That's serious enough, but we'd prefer evidence that he had your father's helicopter shot down or ordered your killing.'

'The person most likely to have done the killings at the Barbican is called Graham Palmer. Palmer definitely shot down my father and ran over my friend Grace, mistaking her for me. Mike confessed this to me. Palmer came after me in Krakow, too. He works for a dirty operations unit that my uncle set up inside Kite Industries.'

'We'll see if we can find out anything about him. This assassin may still be looking for you. Which is another reason why I don't want you near that funeral this afternoon.'

FINCHLEY ROAD, LONDON

Luke cycled to the funeral. Mom said it was a mad thing to do. He wasn't used to London traffic and he would mess up his smart clothes. They reached a compromise whereby Mom took his suit with her and Luke would change at the crematorium.

Megan's bike had arrived from Scotland this morning. It was the same model as Luke had in New York. His sister's bike helmet fitted him fine. He only had to raise the saddle an inch to make the bike a comfortable ride. Riding it felt right, a tribute to his sister. It also gave him an excuse not to ride in the limo with his mom and Mike.

At ten, Luke set off into the city traffic. Soon he was working up a sweat. A lorry had splashed an oily puddle on to his jeans and he was glad that he wasn't in his funeral gear. Avoiding buses and pedestrians who wandered into the bike lanes required concentration. It kept his mind off Megan and what had happened to her. As he neared the cemetery, though, Luke couldn't help but think about what he was going to do.

He'd allowed plenty of time for the journey, so there was still half an hour before the service began. He slacked off a little. A black limousine pulled into the bus and bike lane in front of him, then slowed down. Luke cursed. He was about to cycle around it when he saw a woman in the back waving at him to pull over. Mom. Luke stopped and so did the vehicle. A grey liveried driver got out and opened the vast trunk, which was big enough to take Megan's bike. Mom got out of the car.

'Put your bike in there, Luke. Your uncle needs to talk to you.'

'I don't want to talk to him,' Luke said.

'Why not?'

'You know why! He had Megan killed.'

'Nonsense. It was an accident. Mike wouldn't lie about something like that,' Crystal said.

'And what about the family of the girl who's in the coffin today?' Luke asked. 'Don't they get to bury their daughter?'

'It's only a body,' Crystal argued. 'They had a service to remember her. Today's service is so that people can

229

remember Megan.'

'I'd still like to know exactly how she died,' Luke said.

'There are some things you're better off not knowing,' Crystal repeated.

'Even when I'm in charge of Kite Industries?'

'That's a long way off,' Crystal said. 'When you're ready.'

'I'll never be ready to have people killed,' Luke muttered. How deeply was Mom involved? She'd let Mike pay for her condo in the Village. She was aware that their uncle had had Megan and Maria killed, not to mention a couple of people in London. Did that make Mom an accessory, or whatever the English called it? Would she go to jail?

'If I die before I turn eighteen, Mike inherits everything, right? I can't make a will to change that?'

'You can't. Why would you want to? Mike's on your side.'

'On my side? He had my sister and probably my father killed. Who knows what else he's done. Don't you see, Mom? If we don't turn him in, sooner or later he's bound to turn on us.'

Mom sighed. 'This is why Mike wants to talk to you before the funeral. He thinks you might have something planned. But I swear, he'll never turn on you.'

'Why? Because you're his girlfriend? Don't think I haven't noticed what goes on between you. I know that he's paying for your apartment.'

'It's your apartment too. It'll be very convenient when you start at NYU.'

'I'm not going to university in New York. If I go at all. And I'm not taking Dad's money, not this way. It's immoral!'

'You'll change your mind. There are some things you

230

don't understand.' Mom glared at him. 'You could ruin everything if you shoot your mouth off, Luke. Grow up! Everyone's morals are flexible. Everyone! If you only knew, Mike and I have always thought of you. Always.'

'My sister is dead.'

'She wasn't your sister!' Crystal snapped.

Thirty-Six

HAMPSTEAD CEMETERY, LONDON

The day of Megan's funeral was overcast, muggy. There was no media and there were no flowers, by request. Grace and Ethan were among the first to arrive. They sat in the third row from the front left. Their mother and father would come separately, from Brussels and Westminster. Grace spotted her former head, Mrs Duncan, arriving. She gave Grace a brief wave then sat at the back of the Chapel of Rest. One other girl from school arrived shortly afterwards, Rhianna Belbin. Seeing Grace and Ethan, she joined them.

'Do you know why it's taken so long for this to happen?' Rhianna asked, eyeing up Grace's handsome brother.

'Police,' Grace said, which seemed to satisfy her.

'How's your leg?' Rhianna asked, glancing at Grace's stick.

'I've been told to avoid the pole vault and marathons, but otherwise, I should be completely recovered by Christmas.'

'That's great. It was such a senseless accident.'

Mum and Dad came in, accompanied by a young woman in sunglasses. Ethan, to Grace's surprise, give a start. He seemed to know the girl with the sunglasses and long, very dark hair. The group walked to the front and sat in the row behind Grace, Ethan and Rhianna. Rhianna didn't recognize the girl in sunglasses, but now Grace did. She nodded at her friend, but said nothing. This was going to be interesting.

FINCHLEY ROAD, LONDON

Luke joined his mother and uncle in the black limousine. A bodyguard sat in the front next to the driver. A sound-proof window separated the front from the rear. He wanted his mom to explain herself, but it was Mike who insisted on talking.

'I understand that you have a lot of anxieties about what's been going on. I'd be surprised if you didn't. But you've got to understand one thing, Luke. I've always been ashamed of the way my brother treated you. I know what it's like to be the least favoured child. As soon as Jack was born, our parents favoured him. He was the golden boy, the planned child. You can't begin to imagine how I felt when the company I worked for crashed and I had to go to Jack for a job. It was the final humiliation.'

'The stock market crash wasn't my dad's fault. And It wasn't his fault that my grandparents spoiled him,' Luke pointed out. 'It's certainly wasn't Megan's.'

'The world isn't fair, Luke. This has nothing to do with fault. You only live once. Life's about taking what you can get. And after this funeral takes place, the three of us are home free. Nobody will have any comeback against us, no evidence.'

'What if the real Megan's body shows up?'

Mike hesitated.

'Are you sure that Megan is dead?' Luke asked.

'She died in a car crash which she caused herself.'

'What happened to her body?'

'I don't know!' Mike said. He looked rattled. 'But I was talking to her when it happened. Nobody could have survived that crash. I've got five men keeping an eye on the situation. When we track down her remains, I'll ensure that she gets a proper burial.'

'Under what name?'

'Jane Doe, I suppose. It doesn't matter, Luke. Funerals are for the living. When you're dead, you're dead.'

The limousine had turned into the cemetery. Luke played for time.

'I need to get changed,' he said. He found it hard to look at his uncle. He didn't feel like he really knew him any more. Mike had had his father and his sister killed and why? Greed and jealousy. Sibling rivalry. Stupid stuff.

The car stopped. Luke reached for the door handle.

'Wait,' Crystal said. 'We've been waiting for the right time to tell you something.'

'That the two of you are a couple?' Luke said. 'I worked that out when I saw Mike's name on the lease to the condo. What difference does it make?'

'Your mother and I aren't a couple,' Mike said. 'Though I could understand how you jumped to that conclusion.'

'Mike and I had a thing, but we split up a long time

'ago,' Crystal told her son.

'It must have been a really long time ago, as I don't remember you ever going out with him.'

'It was before you were born,' Mike said.

'Before . . . ?'

'There's no easy way to tell you this,' Crystal said, softly.

Luke worked out what his mom was trying to say. His mouth opened and closed but no words came out.

'Listen carefully,' Mike said. 'Crystal conned my brother into thinking that, one drunken night, he'd got her pregnant. But Jack Kite was not your father.'

'You don't mean . . . ?' Luke tried to ask, but the right words failed him.

Mom took his hand. 'Megan wasn't your sister. She was your cousin.'

Luke turned, wide-eyed, to Mike Kite.

'That's right,' Mike said. 'I'm your dad.'

Thirty-Seven

HAMPSTEAD CEMETERY, LONDON

Mike Kite arrived in the crematorium. With him was Megan's brother, Luke, wearing a black suit, and an attractive, tanned woman, presumably Luke's mother. She wore a matching, low-cut outfit with hat and veil. Which was a bit over the top, Grace thought, given that she wasn't related to Megan. Behind those three was a man in sunglasses who looked worryingly familiar. He remained at the side of the chapel, scoping the surroundings. A bodyguard, presumably. Where had Grace seen him before? The three family members took the empty pew at the front right of the crematorium.

The raven-haired young woman wearing wrap-around sunglasses chose this moment to leave the pew behind, slide past Rhianna, then position herself between Ethan and Grace. It was bright outside, so she wasn't the only mourner wearing sunglasses. Nobody gave her a second look. The other mourners would assume the girl was one of Megan's school-friends. Only the Thompson family knew different.

'They didn't recognize you?' Grace whispered.

'No,' Megan whispered back. 'I was terrified when I saw that guy with them, though. He's Graham Palmer, the guy who ran you over. I don't think he clocked me.'

The service began.

'We are here today to honour the life of a young person whose time on this earth was cut tragically short . . .'

Luke half listened to what was said about Megan, but took little in. This whole day was a farce. They were mourning a girl who might not be dead and who wasn't his sister. Luke couldn't get used to his dad not being his dad. But he knew it was true. As soon as Mom said it, the story made sense. Mike had been there when he was growing up. Jack hadn't. The family resemblance convinced Jack that Luke was his, so the poor sap never even considered a DNA test.

Luke had to admire his uncle's – no, his *father*'s – cunning. He had fathered a child but made his more successful younger brother pay for it, in every sense. Luke used to feel sorry for his abandoned mother, but now he felt terrible for Jack. He had been cheated and used, then killed by his own brother.

What did all this make Luke? His father's son. And still, potentially, a billionaire. Having so much money was obscene, but even if he only kept a small percentage of it, Luke would be rich. He would have a very easy life and he could make a lot of difference as soon as he turned eighteen. He could devote himself to worthy charities. Megan would understand.

No. He couldn't let Mike get away with what he'd done. And yet. Give Mike up, and Luke would be alone in the world. No family, no home. He would probably lose his inheritance, since he wasn't really Jack's son. Whereas, if he stuck with Mike, he'd be rich, beyond anyone's wildest dreams. It was easy to say you hated money when you had none, but Luke knew that what Mom said earlier was true. Everyone's morals were flexible. Everyone. Even priests, like the one speaking now.

'. . . So, as we commit our sister Megan to the glorious hereafter, let us pray.'

The coffin began to move towards the curtain. A song, supposedly one of Megan's favourites, began to play in the background. Luke wanted to vomit. He hated Coldplay.

That was it, Megan decided. They had their proof. She wasn't going to let all of these people think that she was dead. The police had the chapel surrounded. It was safe to reveal herself. Before the funeral ended, she would step forward and . . .

And it was too late. Her brother had beaten her to it.

'Stop the cremation!' he shouted. 'That isn't Megan in there!'

Crystal tried to put her arms around Luke, pull him back, but he wasn't having any of it.

'He's upset!' Crystal said, as her son pushed her away. 'He doesn't know what he's saying.'

'You've lied to me all your life!' he yelled at his mother, as somebody turned off the whingeing music. 'This is all your fault, you and Mike. Your fault that Maria died. Your fault that Da . . . that Jack Kite died, too. Mike had him shot down.'

'You don't know what you're saying,' Crystal said. 'Calm down, we'll talk about this later. I'll take you home.'

Luke wasn't listening to her. He was addressing the mourners, who remained in place, glued to the show. The coffin had halted, its rear still poking out of the red curtains. Mike Kite still stood in the front right pew. He was trying to look calm but his leg was twitching, the way Dad's used to when he was mad about something but didn't want to show it.

'I don't know if Megan's dead or not,' Luke told the mourners. 'I know that Mike Kite tried to have her killed. He had his own brother killed too. And you want to know the sick thing? He didn't just do it for himself, he did it for me. Because, according to these two . . .' he spread his arms, pointing at Crystal and Mike, '. . . they're my parents. Jack Kite was duped into thinking that I was his. And so was I.'

Megan watched Luke begin to cry. She'd never seen him cry before, not even when he was a kid. Crystal stood in frozen horror. Mike hurried down the aisle. Then he stopped, seeing the uniformed police who lined the exit. Megan pushed her way into the aisle, brushed past Mike and joined her brother.

'It's OK,' she told him. 'I'm here. I'm alive. And it doesn't matter what they told you. I'm still your sister.'

She pointed at the bodyguard in the sunglasses, who, like Mike, was trying to get out of the chapel.

'That's the man who killed my father. His name's Graham Palmer. He tried to kill me too, twice, at Mike's command. He murdered Tom Morris and the girl whose body is in that coffin.'

Palmer dashed for the exit but the police had him covered. As they handcuffed him, Megan heard gasps from behind her, and people repeating her name as though trying to convince themselves of what they were seeing. Luke wiped his eyes and stared at her. Megan smiled at him and then, in the silent church, turned to her uncle.

'I'm looking forward to seeing how you get out of this,' she said, with a wry smile.

Mike Kite opened and closed his mouth. Then he made a run for it.

Thirty-Eight

LONDON, ONE MONTH LATER

It was funny, being in the back of the limousine on her own. Megan had hardly spent any time alone since her 'funeral'. Ethan had offered to come with her this afternoon, but her business with the family solicitor was private. She had discussed what she was going to do with Grace and Ethan and their parents, but the decision was entirely hers.

They stopped in traffic near Bond Street. Her chauffeur slid open the window that divided her from him.

'We'll be there in five minutes, ma'am.'

After the funeral, Megan had moved in with the Thompsons. She felt like an adopted daughter, except that she was having a thing with the only son and adopted daughters weren't meant to do that. Impossible to guess how long she and Ethan would last. It didn't matter. He was gentle and kind and funny, which was more than enough to be going on with.

Today was her birthday. She'd wanted to delay having a party until after the A-level results, but Grace said that that was a bad idea. What if their results were rubbish? She wouldn't want a party then. And you only turned eighteen once. So she'd agreed to a small, select group of friends. Luke was coming over from the States for the celebration.

The business at the solicitor's was a formality. They had discussed everything that needed to be done a couple of weeks ago, but the papers couldn't be signed until she reached her eighteenth birthday. In the course of five minutes, Megan would put her name to everything, in triplicate, using her best, most ornate handwriting. Then there would be no going back.

'New Scotland Yard please,' Luke told the taxi driver at Heathrow.

He had promised Ian Trevelyan that he would stop by before going to Islington, for Megan's eighteenth. The journey there was slow but oddly relaxing. Returning to London brought back a lot of memories, not all of them bad.

It still gave Luke pleasure to think about Mike Kite's downfall. He'd followed Mike out of the crematorium. His uncle found the path to his limousine blocked by uniformed officers. So he grabbed Megan's bike, which Luke had earlier propped against the side of the building. Awkwardly, he mounted the machine and attempted to cycle away. But Mike was overweight and clumsy and not used to riding a bike. He wobbled so much that it was painful to watch, almost comic. The police caught him within seconds.

Mike had been extradited to the US, where he was resident when all of the crimes took place. He had committed no murders himself, but the evidence on Jimmy Quigley's cellphone was enough to tie him to the death of

Maria Delgado and the attempts on Megan's life. His cover-up of the two killings at the Barbican also indicated his involvement in them, but proving that he had commissioned those killings, along with Jack Kite's murder, was going to be more difficult.

It was nearly six before he reached New Scotland Yard.

'I can't stay long,' Luke warned Ian Trevelyan. 'I'm late for a party.'

'Please give Megan my regards. She's had a very tough time. She deserves to have some fun.'

'What did you want to see me about?' Luke asked. 'Have the FBI changed their minds? Are they going to try and make me testify against my mom?'

'No, it's not that. Are you still not talking to your mother?'

'What would be the point? I can never believe a thing she says any more.'

'I know what you mean,' Trevelyan said. 'But you only have one mother, no matter how irresponsible she may be.'

Luke nodded impatiently. He might reconcile with Crystal one day, but it would be in his own sweet time. 'Why did you call me in, Ian?'

'We ran DNA tests on your uncle and your sister.'

'So? You warned me that it's hard to prove the cousin relationship through DNA.'

'That's true. Except you and Megan are not cousins,' Trevelyan said.

What next? Luke thought. 'Let me guess. You're going to tell me that Megan and I aren't actually related. My mum lied to everyone.'

'Not at all. Your mother lied to you about many things. She may have lied to your uncle about your paternity. Probably she had affairs with both Kite brothers and didn't know which of them was your father. So she told both of them that you were theirs. Mike Kite thought he was conning his brother, but it was Crystal who was conning him, whether she knew it or not. The DNA test was conclusive. Jack Kite was your father. Megan is your sister.'

Luke sighed. He'd tried to tell himself that not having a sister didn't matter, but he felt a great sense of relief.

'Have you told Megan?'

'I thought you might prefer to do that yourself.'

The solicitor took the papers from her.

'That's signed and sealed, then. You'll cede one half of your Kite Industries shares to Luke Kite on his eighteenth birthday,' the solicitor said. 'He's a lucky young man.'

'Both of his parents are in prison, awaiting trial,' Megan pointed out. 'I wouldn't say he's all that lucky.'

They were finished. Megan shook the solicitor's hand and returned to her car. The chauffeur held the door open and Megan got in. Her bodyguard, meanwhile, stood back from the road, surveying the scene. Satisfied, he got into the front passenger seat of the bullet-proofed car.

'Kite Building, ma'am?' the chauffeur asked.

'No. Take me home, please.'

Megan fastened her seat belt. Security would not always need to be as tight as this, Ian Trevelyan had assured her. The vast majority of Kite Industries employees were loyal to Megan and to her father's memory. Now that she had inherited, there was no immediate threat. Thanks to Jimmy Quigley's phone records, the police had good intelligence on who was in the Kite 'dirty squad' that Mike had set up and used against her and her dad. Three had already been arrested, all of them in New York.

Megan hadn't told Luke about his share of the inheritance, not yet. She hoped he'd be pleased. There was more than enough money for both of them, but Megan knew that money alone didn't make you happy. She'd give it all up to have either of her parents back. And Luke would probably give it all away for the chance to change his.

Money was also a big responsibility. Megan's gap year would now be spent learning how their company worked. She hoped that Luke would want to join in, but he might have had enough of the whole thing. She wouldn't blame him. No, she would blame him. He was her brother, or the nearest thing to a brother that she would ever have. She needed his help.

The limo pulled up in the Thompsons' Islington street. The bodyguard scoped the surroundings then signalled that it was safe for Megan to get out. There were more cars in the street than usual. It was dusk and the small party was not due to start until nine, or so she'd been told. But Megan could see balloons through the window and suspected that everyone was already there. The whole thing would kick off the minute she walked through the door.

Nothing could surprise her any more.

Look out for:

Kite Identity: Book Two

BAD COMPANY
Harry Edge

Luke's sister Megan is in danger again, and Luke realises his power as part owner of Kite Industries means nothing when he cannot be sure who, or what, is holding Megan to ransom . . .

And then there is his dad's ex-girlfriend, who seems friendly enough, but has a strong motive to be rid of both Megan and Luke.

Luke wants to believe that he can trust his own flesh and blood above all else. But he's beginning to realise that no one is beyond suspicion.

A tense action thriller introducing two unforgettable sibling heroes.